THE ANIMATED SKELETON

D1440838

Gothic Classics

THE
ANIMATED SKELETON

BY
ANONYMOUS

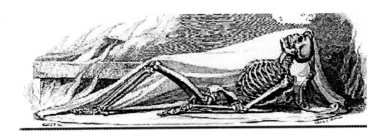

VALANCOURT BOOKS
CHICAGO

Published by Valancourt Books
Chicago, Illinois

Originally published in 1798
First published by Valancourt Books, February 2005
Second Valancourt Books printing, August 2005

Cover design by Ryan Cagle

The Animated Skeleton
ISBN 0-9766048-0-9
Library of Congress Control Number: 2005920880

Printed in the United States of America

CONTENTS

FOREWORD

Most readers interested in Gothic fiction are familiar with the famous titles of that period, such as Horace Walpole's *The Castle of Otranto*, Ann Radcliffe's *The Mysteries of Udolpho*, and M. G. Lewis's *The Monk*. It may, then, seem a bit odd that an editor would choose a minor work, like *The Animated Skeleton*, as the inaugural volume of a series called "Gothic Classics."

But in many ways, books like *Otranto, Udolpho*, and *The Monk*, are unrepresentative of the genre as a whole. Walpole and Lewis were members of Parliament, and neither they, nor Mrs. Radcliffe, wrote out of need for money. Most Gothic novelists of the period, by contrast, wrote for their bread; their very livelihoods depended on the success of their novels. And many of these writers, whose texts fed the public's insatiable hunger for Gothic fiction, were quite successful.

About the author of *The Animated Skeleton*, nothing is known. The book was published anonymously by William Lane's Minerva Press in two volumes in 1798. The Minerva was the great purveyor of Gothic fiction during the period between 1790 and 1820; about half of these Gothic novels, like *The Animated Skeleton*, were published anonymously. Female authors were more likely to wish to maintain their anonymity, since it was still seen as shameful in some circles for women to write romances, although some male authors preferred to conceal their identities as well, particularly if they doubted the success of their book.

The present novel is quite remarkable in a number of ways. Although its ending recalls the style of Mrs. Radcliffe, *The Animated Skeleton* is hardly, like many other novels of the period, a cheap imitation of her work. Rather, it has an unusual style and mood all its own, mixing fairly standard elements of Gothic horror with a unique flavour of dark humour. The novel's gloomy opening, in evoking real suspense and terror, contrasts sharply with later scenes, such as the one where the ghost taunts Grimoald in an episode which cannot but be described as slapstick comedy.

Professor Frederick S. Frank, in his book *The First Gothics*, described *The Animated Skeleton* as one of the best of the many novels written in imitation of Mrs. Radcliffe's style, and praised its ability to maintain a level of real suspense and true supernatural. His is hardly the first study of Gothic literature to discuss *The Animated Skeleton*; mention of it occurs in almost every major work on the subject. It is then surprising that a novel as entertaining and historically important as *The Animated Skeleton* has remained out of print since its first publication.

Valancourt Books is proud to present, for the first time in over two centuries, the first in its series of Gothic Classics: *The Animated Skeleton.*

JAMES D. JENKINS
Seattle, February 2005

A NOTE ON THE TEXT

This edition follows the text of the original edition, published in 1798 by William Lane's Minerva Press. There has been no attempt to modernize or standardize spelling or punctuation. The author alternates between spellings of some words (e.g., "surprize," and "surprise") and misspells some words consistently (e.g., "teize" for "tease"); these variations have been maintained in this edition. Obvious misprints and particularly confusing typographical elements, such as the sometimes inconsistent use of quotation marks, have been silently corrected only where necessary for clarity.

THE

ANIMATED

SKELETON

—➤➤◆◄—

IN TWO VOLUMES.

═══════════

" .... I oft have fought,
" With friendly tender of fome worthier fervice,
" To win him from his temper, but he fhuns
" All offers——
" .... Is there caufe for this?
" For fin without temptation, calm cool villany—
" Deliberate mifchief, unimpaffioned luft,
" And fmiling murder———"

GUSTAVUS VASA.

═══════════

VOL. I.

═══════════════════

LONDON:

PRINTED AT THE

Minerva-Prefs,

FOR WILLIAM LANE, LEADENHALL-STREET.

1798.

PREFACE

THE fashionable style of Novels has been for some time dressed in the garb of fiction; and the title of "a story founded on facts," has been universally received with pleasure.

I pretend not here to produce facts for my foundation: through the regions of imagination only have I strayed to gather those materials which arose spontaneously, whichever way I moved. To me it has ever appeared, that turning truth into romance was divesting it of its real charms. The stomach long habituated to the high-seasoned dish, turns with dislike and loathing, from the plain and wholesome food. The gloss of fiction leads astray the mind, and when a fact is mentioned, it only recollects as is ornamented by the romantic writer. It is not to be supposed a very young person will give up the sweet and alluring recitals of a Reeve, a White, or a Lee, to travel through a Smollet, a Hume, or a Rapin. Ask them whence they would draw their historic information, and they lead you to the windings of a Recess, or present you to the Knight of the Face. Perhaps, with Richard Coeur de Lion, they produce a black cat, or, when speaking of his return from imprisonment, exclaim, "Oh aye, it was then he met with the Hero of the Pitcher."

I am well convinced that History can receive no additional beauty from fiction, nor have I the presumption to think I am capable of giving it any, could it be received from art. If my story has any merit, it consists in its brevity, in its being entirely invention, and without a sentiment intended to corrupt the heart.

The reign of Hugh Capet presented to my mind the overgrown power of the nobles; and there alone have I glanced at reality, except in attempting to adapt my story to the manners of the times.

If my sentiments are erroneous, let it be imputed to an unformed judgment and a powerless pen, which has never been directed by a wish to injure.

Now I pray you, good readers, do not quarrel with the kitten, which plays its unoffending antics to divert you — it is the best it can do: — its abilities are not equal to its will; and if you have more rationality, that is your happiness, not the kitten's fault; be pleased then with its intention, and pardon its weakness.

COUNT RICHARD;

OR,

THE ANIMATED SKELETON

DISMALLY was the tempest howling round the cottage of Jacquemar; the snow beat in at the osier watling, which served for windows: it fell on the ill-formed roof, and melted through it. The infant sons of the peasant crept close to their father, half terrified and nearly cold. "Do, papa, wrap us in your cloke, and keep us warm," cried the eldest:—'Tell us a story,' said the youngest, 'until mamma comes home, and gives us some victuals. Why don't she come?' "Alas," replied Jacquemar, whose bosom was filled with anxiety for the return of his Dunisleda, "my love, I know not; she went to seek provisions; and if not more fortunate than usual, you will be obliged to go to sleep without a supper. Perhaps she is staying to procure some money." 'Why do not you go and bring her home, papa?' "My dear child, she went to sell some cheese, but I know not whither she turned."— The sound of a person who tried to enter at the wicket-door of the cottage, made the hearts of the children beat quick with hope and joy. 'Oh, it is mamma! it is mamma!'—"Ah, my dears, she would enter immediately;

1

but I will go and see."—The cottage of Jacquemar was divided into two rooms; one in which they slept and lived; and a smaller one, in which they penned a goat: the entrance into the dwelling being through the smaller, they could not discover who was coming; but on arriving at the wicket, Jacquemar found it was indeed Dunisleda. Her strength had but just supported her to the door, which she had made an ineffectual effort to open. Cold, fear, and weakness, had rendered her hands too much benumbed to perform their office: that being done by Jacquemar, she attempted to rush in; but before she could accomplish her purpose she fainted on the bosom of her husband. Jacquemar, in his arms, carried her to the fire (which the snow had nearly extinguished) but the sudden alarm and grief that penetrated his heart, prevented his lending her any other assistance. Almost reduced to equal torpor with his wife, he could only press her to his bosom and gaze upon her face, which was bloody; and her clothes were wet and torn. The youngest infant rubbed his mother's hands, to restore their warmth, whilst the weeping eldest raked the few embers on the hearth together, and, after warming his own scanty coverings, crawled up and wrapped them round his mother's shoulders. Long was it before Dunisleda discovered any signs of re-animation; but at length opening her eyes, she drew a sigh; she beheld her husband and children. Surprize first warmed her countenance; the surprize which we feel when after being separated a few moments from the dominions of reason, we return from the illusions of a distempered brain to the regions of reality. Thought returning, she faintly smiled, and softly said, but in an agitated whisper, "Fly,

my Jacquemar, let us fly to some distant cottage imme—
——" The sounds died upon her lips, the effort over-
came her, and she again became insensible. Her
miserable husband and his little ones each uttered a cry
of horror. At that moment a figure rushed in, wrapped
up in a long cloke, and his features covered; 'Fly Jacquemar, fly to the cottage of Grodern; here certain ruin
awaits your stay: fly this instant, and there rest quiet
until you hear further from Alwin.' Not remaining to
listen to their interrogatories, the figure, after having
uttered the above words, swiftly made his exit from
their presence.

"Gracious Parent of the universe," exclaimed Jacquemar, "what can I have done to merit this? and who
can be my enemy?"

Lost in astonishment, he hung over Dunisleda, who
at length began to recover: he entreated her eagerly to
declare the cause of the stranger's advice and appearance, but more, of her own exclamation and mournful
situation. 'Oh my love, cause me not to waste my little
strength in the explanation; let me save it, that, with
your assistance, I may before it is too late, escape to the
cottage of Grodern with my poor little ones! Oh, we
must not delay one moment!'

At that instant entered Grodern himself, attended by
his son.—"My friends," said he, "I am come with Edgar
to assist you in your removal: Alwin has been at my
home, and has sent me hither."

'Who is Alwin?'

"Stay not for questions—Dunisleda, lean on the arm
of your husband, and on my son's; I will lead the children."

3

Exerting her utmost strength, Dunisleda supported as he desired, slowly walked from their dwelling, scarcely able to crawl on, although aided by the two peasants.—The shivering infants could not long creep through the snow; the old man carried the biggest in his arms, and Edgar was obliged to bear the other: thus at last, cold, faint, and weary, they arrived at the hospitable shelter. The ancient wife of Grodern carried Dunisleda to her own bed (which consisted of moss and long dried grass, which they had gathered from the sides of the forest, covered with coarse linen) and quitted the room, that she might not disturb her repose.

The astonished Jacquemar now demanded an explanation; which was only thus partially complied with by Grodern, who addressed him as follows:—"About a quarter of an hour before you saw me, Edward, one of the attendants belonging to the lady of Duke Albert, came into my cottage, and earnestly entreated me to receive you and your family this night, and to hasten and encourage your departure, for that great mischief would befall you if I refused, or even hesitated a few hours. Tell them, added he, if they delay, that Alwin sent you. Although he was disguised, I easily recognized him to be Edward; determining to give him no suspicion, after I had made this discovery, I immediately attended on you."

'Alas! I fear some treachery,' replied Jacquemar; 'the Duke is a great enemy to all the poor vassals in his territories, who have any handsome females belonging to them.—I fear for my poor Dunisleda! and I believe I shall soon be made more miserable, because I love her!'

"Ah, Jacquemar," said the old man, "the Duke is a good prince, and would be the friend of all his poor vassals, if his lady would let him: she is so bad, that I know not whether day or night has been the greatest witness of her atrocities. You must take care and conceal my knowledge of the false Alwin, and also my opinion of his mistress.

"They say those terrible ghosts in the castle are all caused by his great wickedness."

'Rather say, they appear to be in time the discovery of hers. But hush, these are not subjects for the comments of the poor and helpless. Even in my own cottage I shudder, lest being overheard I should draw her anger and vengeance down upon me.

'Perhaps in the morning my Dunisleda may be able to tell who is to be blamed.'

"We must all use our caution; the disguise of Edward calls upon us likewise to be disguised, at least in speech and manner. Under the sway of a bad master, honesty is of no avail with a poor cottager, whose virtues are as silent and solemn monitors against the great man's vices, and are received and treated as high insults would be. When the furious lady of Duke Albert aims at our destruction, subtilty alone opposed to subtilty, can save us from her malice, unless we betake ourselves to immediate flight. I have long been the marked object of her wrath."

'Alas, my friend, what could have been the cause? or how are you enabled to know it?'

"Female depravity is alone the cause of all her bitter enmity; and female worth the partial reason of my knowledge.—But stay, we are wasting time, that appears to me far too precious to be spent in idle conference. A thought strikes me:—to-morrow I will declare my story: but for this night recruit your spirits with a little sleep, and when you have refreshed yourself I will communicate the plan I have already formed."

'Ah, Grodern, my mind is too anxious for sleep: weariness is far away; but fear, wonder, and curiosity, are waking. My suspense is cruel!'

The infants had been long asleep upon the straw and rushes with which the apartment was spread; Grodern wished to follow their example, and, complaining of great fatigue, refused to satisfy the curiosity of Jacquemar; who being constrained at last by the laws of hospitality, suffered the others to enjoy that repose which he denied himself, and waited until day-break in a state of unspeakable distress and anxiety. At day-light Grodern arose from his sleep, and thus bespoke the eager eared Jacquemar:—

"My friend, our lives and liberties appear to me in danger here: I know of a temporary safeguard: the abbess of a neighbouring convent is my benefactress and unshaken friend. I lived under the same roof with her father, and shared her infant play: time severed us, but time has never obliterated from her memory the days of childhood, or from her heart the sweet ties of innocent and youthful amity. Towards her then, ere it is morning, let us all bend our footsteps, and seek the mansion of hospitality and benevolence: She will receive and protect us until we hear more, and can plan better; but before I introduce you, first promise never to enquire of me or seek to discover my method of receiving intelligence: it would injure us greatly were it discovered: you have only to rest satisfied, and you will be well. Let us awake Dunisleda, and after some refreshment is taken, we will depart to the convent."

Fortunately for the refugees, there had fallen a heavy rain in the latter part of the night, which entirely thawed the snow, so as to prevent their route being discovered by the marks of their footsteps. The scheme of Grodern soon obtained the consent of the whole party; and after a hasty meal, made on some poor cheeses, milk, and barley-cakes, they prepared to set out on their walk. "We must pass in silence through the forest," said Grodern, "lest some early spy or wily deceiver should overhear our converse, and betray our departure; and I doubt not but the emissaries of Brunchilda will be early at our cottages."

'When we have passed the forest, wherefore cannot you tell me the history of her anger, which you last night promised me? and why will it not then be safe to listen to Dunisleda?' peevishly asked the impatient Jacquemar.

Dunisleda declared she could not support the walk and the cold of the weather, if obliged to give her narration during the one, or until relieved from the other; "besides," added Grodern, "by the warm cheering fire of the hospitable convent, we may converse in safety and in comfort:—we may sit unmoved by the surrounding storm, and look back unterrified on the past."

They accordingly departed in silence; but the cold of the morning which was doubly felt when they had left the shelter of the forest, was almost too much for the enfeebled Dunisleda and her tender offspring. 'Bear up my love,' cried Jacquemar, 'the convent must be near at hand.' "Alas," replied the shivering partner of his way, "I have ventured too much: my strength is too far exhausted to suffer me to survive the shock of last night's terrors or this morning's walk!"

Poor Dunisleda had reason to complain of the severity of the weather: she felt the pangs of child-birth approaching: the fears of the preceding evening had brought them on. In pain and sorrow she dragged her suffering frame towards the convent; at six in the morning, at dim distance, they beheld its towers; scarcely would they have been perceptible had not a high hill, on whose bleak sides the snow lay yet unmelted, been at a distance behind the convent, by which the contrast of the black towers were shewn.—'Now then we are safe,' exclaimed Grodern, 'from the tyranny of Brunchilda; cheer up, cheer up, Dunisleda; see the abbey-lights!'—

"Cursed villain!" roared a voice from behind him, "you are safe; safe in my power, safe in my detection!" At that instant he received a wound from a dagger, and starting round, by the light of a dark lantern which the villain held in his hand, he perceived Conrad, a favourite with Brunchilda. Jacquemar instantly, on hearing a shriek of surprise from Grodern, and beholding the miscreant, flew on him with the rage of a tiger, and, wresting the dagger from his grasp, plunged it deep in the bosom of the assassin. He fell; and, uttering blasphemous execrations, died. Dunisleda gave a loud scream, and fainted in the arms of Edgar. She had seen Grodern bleed; and instant fear made her apprehend a numerous party was at hand.—She could not sustain it, but became insensible.

"This, this is ruin," cried Grodern, unmindful of his bleeding shoulder, which happily, however, was but slightly hurt; "we must remove the body, or we shall by that be traced. You, Edgar and Jacquemar, must assist me to convey it to the convent."

'Alas! my Dunisleda, my Dunisleda, I must attend to her,' replied the anxious Jacquemar.—Grodern now, with redoubled vexation, beheld the insensible state of the unfortunate female. "Alas!" said he, "we must convey her to the convent as we can; my son must remain and bury the body. Speed forward Edgar, and borrow such instruments as are necessary to secure Conrad's corpse in the earth, safe from observation: we must not attempt to drag it on, lest the blood should betray us. "

Edgar hastened forward; and meanwhile the sorrowing party slowly conveyed Dunisleda within the gates; a good fire and attention soon restored her to her senses—but immediately the pangs of parturition seized her with redoubled force, and she was shortly after delivered of a dead child. The tenderest care was shewn her by the abbess, the nuns, and the wife of Grodern; yet there appeared but little hopes of her recovery to any of them.

After some time Edgar returned from the interment of Conrad's body—nothing had occurred to prevent him, and he believed he was perfectly secure from discovery. The snow beginning again to fall, covered the place where he had deposited the villain, and at the same time hid the blood which had flowed from his wound.

Sorrow now for the sufferings of his wife entirely repressed the curiosity of Jacquemar; his Dunisleda was for many days unable to speak; but at last, knowing her husband's anxiety, she strove to address him: her attendants attempted to prevent her, and on account of her debilitated state, enjoined her a strict silence; but as soon as better enabled, she declared to them it was of little use; for although she might be more exhausted by speaking just then, yet it was of no moment, as she felt she could never recover.—Death had marked her for his own, and would not be disappointed. A temporary renovation she might feel, but the cold and terror had too deeply affected her, ever to suffer her to be radically cured, or indeed to let her live any length of time. Having regained, by the assistance of their cordials, a small degree of strength, she told Jacquemar she would relate to him her adventure of the preceding evening, as it might be of great consequence to hear it recited by herself. As soon therefore as he would permit her, she thus told what he anxiously listened to.

The Escape of Dunisleda.

"You know, my Jacquemar, I left my cottage early in the morning, to sell the few cheeses I had made. I departed for the nearest village to the dwelling of Duke Albert; hoping that in the neighbourhood of the castle I should have more chance of vending my little store, and thereby sustain my starving infants. Perhaps, said I to myself, I may in the walks near that building meet my dear benefactress, the Lady Hildegarda; she will hear, and pity our misfortunes. As I was proceeding, a young man overtook and asked me whither I was walking; and on hearing, said he was going the same way. He would walk on with me and talk. I did not wish for his company, and tried to be silent; but he asked me so many questions, I could not. At last he asked me if I had seen the Duke often? I told him I had never seen him: then, said he, you would not know if a person spoke to you, whether it was the Duke or not? I still replied no! Well, said he, you must beware of him; he is a very wicked man: every woman that is beautiful becomes his prey;— he sets men to discover if any poor man has a beautiful wife or daughter.—Ah, said I, I have heard he is bad, but I am safe; for though my husband calls me beautiful, I know that is only because his love makes him like my face better than others; besides, it is not such beauty as mine pleases great people, they like fair ladies who are shut up in castles, and look white: poverty is also my defence; scarcely can I purchase such articles of wear as are necessary, much less such as would make me shine forth to catch a Prince's eye — You are wrong, replied he; the Duke knows better than to court the sickly slender females you describe. — Knows better, Sir! I mean (quick he returned) despises them; he seeks those lasses whose faces seem to have stolen the bloom of spring, and whose mouths breathe all its fragrance—such as thee, sweet fair.—I fear, Sir, by your talk, you are worse than the Duke, and am ashamed to be seen with you.—You do me great wrong; I can see and protect, but can never injure beauty;—but I see the poverty of your clothes will serve in the Duke's eye as a foil to your charms, which must shine the brighter from the contrast. But some people tell me different of Duke Albert: they say he is the father of the fatherless, and protector of the poor.— Oh very true, he is so more especially if they are fe- males: he generally protects them in a part of his castle

11

set apart for the purpose, and said to be haunted; but I believe it is chiefly with she-spirits.—I did not know whether I should believe him or not; but he begged if I meant to come home late in the evening, to let him see me safe home, or go round another way. I told him I did not desire his company, and bade him leave me. This he soon after did, saying the time might come when I should wish for his assistance. I went on to the village, and was very lucky: so I set off again, thinking of my little ones all the while; but I came back the same way, because it was the safest at night. I beheld nobody until I came near the side of the forest; there I saw two men standing behind a large tree. I was frightened, and scarcely dared to walk on. When I came more near, they rushed forwards, and, seizing me roughly by the arm, attempted to drag me to the forest.—I resisted whilst I was able, but in vain; and they were bearing me forcibly away. One of them cursed me for screaming, and said the Count will pay us handsomely for this lovely creature.—What do you mean by calling Albert the Count? said the other.—Well, well, the Duke.—My continued screams brought a man to my assistance, who came running to me with his sword drawn. My weakness, from fatigue, and the pain I suffered from the bruises I received by their roughness, joined with my fear, made me faint. When I recovered, I found myself supported by my deliverer, in whom I discovered the young man who had given me his advice in the morning. He now reproached me with my former ill opinion of him, and said he hoped I should in future pay more attention to his cautions. I felt very much ashamed of myself, and begged his pardon: he said he could not now attend me home, because he would go in pursuit of the men who had fled, just before I recovered; but bade me to run home directly; and desired I would not disbelieve him any more. I readily promised to obey him. It now was become nearly dark, from the lateness of the evening, and a heavy storm drawing over the forest, made it become quite so. The snow and rain which began to fall chilled me, and I lost my way several times before I reached our door: and this, my dear Jacquemar, is the cause of all you have seen; but I must not forget to tell you, the young man bid me remember Alwin."

Here Dunisleda concluded; and exhausted with the effort, requested they would leave her, as she felt weary, and wished for repose. They therefore quitted the cell where she then lay.

"Good heavens!" said Jacquemar, when they were seated, "what must my poor love have suffered! But noble, noble Alwin, how shall I ever repay his care! how ever express my gratitude!"

'You know not the value of gratitude,' said Grodern, 'if you cast it away on so execrable a villain!'

"Unjust old man, my gratitude is due to my wife's preserver!"

'Dim-sighted youth! your wife's sure murderer! you make gratitude become a vice, to bestow it on those base men who, to gain their own ends, pretend to serve you!'

"Oh, Grodern, he was generous, brave, and noble."

'Jacquemar, he is a villain! but alas, how is youth deceived by the outward appearance! the honesty of the good render them more obnoxious to the knavery of the wicked. You, poor Jacquemar, are the dupe of art.'

"Wherefore called you him my wife's murderer?"

'He is no less.—Observed you what your Dunisleda said of the two men? the mistake of the Count for the Duke.'

"I did."

'Knowest thou not Count Hubert?'

"Ha! Grodern! how dare you call him by that name! it has long been declared a matter of death to name him so. Count Richard is now his title."

'How long, Jacquemar, has this order been?'

"Ever since the wicked Count Richard fled from the old court, and I was a little boy then; but several have been taken since, and sent we know not whither, for calling him Hubert."

Grodern at this showed strong marks of anger and surprise on his countenance, and became gloomy and lost in thought.

In about an hour's time Dunisleda sent for Jacquemar: she had awaked low and very ill.

Jacquemar in vain essayed to cheer her spirits. He chatted, he sung softly to her: once the sound of his voice would raise her; once the wild notes of a rustic instrument he played on, would inspire her with life. The charm was lost, she became more low, and talked of dying. Jacquemar still sung to please his Dunisleda; but his notes savoured of strong melancholy. He was ill in spirits at her sufferings, his words soon caught the infection, and he could only sing according to the impulse of the occasion:

Cheerily, cheerily,
Smile, smile, dear love, smile cheerily.
No more is heard the northern blast;
The storm is spent, the tempest past:
Smile like yon sun, smile cheerily.

In a faint voice, to his great but painful surprise, she replied,

Cheerily, cheerily,
I never must smile cheerily;
For though the wint'ry storm is past,
Too rude too rough has been the blast;
And life it drags on wearily, wearily!
Yet would thy Dunisleda stay,
Cheer thee one hour, and then away,
would fate permit:
But no! My love, forget thy grief;
Let thy fond infants bring relief,
as most is fit:
'Tis thou that must smile cheerily.

Her voice failed her, and she sunk back on the couch. He thought she had only closed her eyes from weakness, he knew not she had fainted; but pained by her reply, he with streaming eyes, whilst he eagerly pressed her chilly hands, continued,

Drearily, drearily;
Life will but pass too drearily!
Arise, my Dunisleda, smile,
One look, sad sorrow to beguile.

15

Oh speak, smile, breathe—Oh God! speak—
Dunisled!—Oh Dunisled, Dunisled!—Gracious Heavens!—my love, my love!—Speak to me, Dunisled——

Dunisleda spoke not: he raised her, he kissed her.
Her lips grew cold, she chilled upon his bosom!—a small
noise in her throat; she opened her mouth!—Half ago-
nized with hope and fear, he again cried, My love, speak.
She spoke not: he gently shook her. Speak, Dunisled.—
Short breathing, he gazed in frigid horror; but she had
not opened her mouth to speak. Life, no longer willing
to animate her body, departed rudely, and in the shock
caused her jaw-bone to descend. The starting of her
eyes taught her Jacquemar his fate!

Let me close the door of the cell on the sorrows of
the mourner; the contemplation of his sufferings cannot
be agreeable to the reader. Let us leave him to the mel-
iorating hand of Time, though we must sigh for him,
whilst we say with the sweet sonneteer,

> But ah! what pain must that poor heart endure,
> That hopes from thee, and thee alone, a cure!
>
> BOWLES.

On the evening of the day on which the remains of
Dunisleda were interred, Grodern, who had been absent
much of the time since their arrival at the convent, returned, and informed Jacquemar it was not proper
longer to indulge in his sorrows: it was his duty as well
as his interest to rouse his firmness, and prepare for the
occurrences of the ensuing day.

"To-morrow," said he, "the convent will be searched.
Brunchilda is certain we are here: she will, in the Duke's
name, demand us. If we are not given up, she will by

16

force attempt to find us." 'Perhaps, Grodern, you can inform us what has passed since we left the forest.' "I can. On the morning of our flight a complaint was laid before the Duke that you and myself, assisted by my son, had attacked two of Brunchilda's attendants, and had attempted to murder them, but they were rescued by Edward. It was said we immediately fled homewards. Messengers were dispatched therefore to our cottages to arrest us; but we were not to be found: their enquiries were equally unsuccessful; no one had seen us since the overnight, when we had spoken to many; who declared, on their being questioned, that we showed no signs of a predetermined flight. Conrad had been out early in the morning, and never returned again: the accusers there-fore hesitated not to say, we had murdered and concealed him. Brunchilda mourned his loss greatly; for, excepting Edward, that wicked woman had not a greater favourite amongst her domestics."

'Is it a crime then to have a favourite?'

"A virtuous friendship, Jacquemar, stimulates its possessors to be good and great; but virtue is unknown to the lady of Duke Albert, who lavishes on every base usurper the affections due only to her lord. Let the thick bowers of the garden of Albert declare the wickedness of Brunchilda, and the insolence of Conrad. — Greatly was the lady enraged at our departure; she in vain tried to account for it; she could not discover our reasons. Sometimes she said to her privy council, that she feared we had received some intelligence from them of her designs, and thus were enabled to counteract her plans. Jealousy reigned amongst them for several days,—and she shunned their advice; but at length, striving to forget it, wishing again for their favour, and being determined to find us, she again consulted them. Passing over the way we came by, one of her household saw a dead body lying on the ground: it appeared to have been torn up from a hole which was fresh and near it. It was wounded in the bosom, and appeared to have been murdered: it had no covering whatever; and already the birds of prey were hovering over it. The body appeared to have been many days deprived of life; but the extreme coldness of the weather had prevented it from becoming putrid.

"The man examined it, and was going away, when the countenance arrested his attention. After a minute's survey, he found it to be Conrad's. — I cannot account otherwise for its being above ground, than that some person whose notice was attracted by seeing the newly-dug earth, after the melting of the snow, had the curiosity to examine the place; and finding a body well clothed, stripped it of its covering.—Big with his discovery, the man went home and immediately imparted the news to Brunchilda. For some time she was at a loss to account for his death, until she recollected the road by which he was found led to the convent. She then called to mind the great kindness of the abbess to all the poor cottagers around;—and she fancied we had flown hither for protection. To-morrow therefore we are to be sought for. She has now charged us with the murder and robbery.—Conrad's body is shown the Duke as a proof thereof; and he believes our calumniators.— Disguise must be our refuge, for innocence will not alone do. Our flight looks suspicious; besides, there was no impartial witness to declare that we only acted from self-defence. The wound in my shoulder will be ridiculed; we must therefore go through in the manner we set out:—my wife shall wear the habit of an ancient nun, and we will appear as monks from a neighbouring monastery. To the abbess we must trust for the concealment of the children."

'Good Grodern, how can they dare to search a convent! What right have they for so sacriligious an act?'

"Ask not by what right they do it:—power, with them, is sufficient right: but besides, the overgrown power of our nobles cannot be retrenched; long has it been the burden of the people: vainly have they appealed to their monarch; he is but a noble with a more sounding title. If the monarch offers to restrain them, or question their behaviour, he receives in return some rebellious answer or insolent demeanor; and Hugh Capet is but a King of Wood, set up for men to gaze at, not obey!"

'Cannot the convent apply to the pope, or threaten them with his vengeance?'

"No, Jacquemar, for they despise the latter, whilst they would prevent the first. Should we be discovered, we shall be tried, condemned, and executed by the adherents of Brunchilda."—

After this Grodern was silent for some time. Jacquemar having paused a while on the danger of the morrow, suffered his thoughts to revert to the melancholy subject they had been drawn from. Used to hard and continual labour in all weathers,—uneducated, and unable to read, how could the mind of a peasant be amused for a number of days, when deprived of his usual employment! Jacquemar until now had scarcely had a grief. If misfortune did gently oppress him, his constant work, or the soothing of his Dunisleda, made him forget his care. Here he had nothing to do: living in ease and plenty, without the necessity of labour to procure a subsistence, might please the dreamer of a little space; but in idleness our peasant could only nourish grief: and he fell into a long and painful depth of thought and retrospection. Grodern with pity beheld his suffering; and he attempted to amuse him.

"Jacquemar," said he, "I will tell you something which happened last night at the castle; it may serve to convince you the northern wing is not inhabited by the Duke's she-spirits. There arrived lately a knight from the court of England, called Sir Raymond Fitz-Henry: he is now at the castle. The party at the same place was last night augmented by the arrival of a stranger knight, in black armour. Every thing he had about him was black, except what I proceed to describe:—He carried a shield covered with cloth of the same dismal hue. On being asked what were his bearings, he removed the black cloth, and showed that his shield was covered with another painted one. 'Beneath this,' said he, 'they are; but never until a certain deed is done shall it be removed; then shall my cognizance be seen, and then shall my name be known. Until then, call me Grimoaldus the Avenger.'

The painting on the second covering of his shield consisted of a dark ground: on it was depicted a female who had just wounded and killed an old stork, which lay dead at her feet. From its bosom was issuing a young serpent, which was beginning to wind its body round the feet of the woman: it had given her a deadly wound;

and she appeared to be agitated by great pain and rage. She seemed in vain to strive to withdraw herself from, or shake off the venomous animal.

The knight was attended by no squire or page: he is a noble and majestic figure; Brunchilda views him with a look of curiosity and admiration. Sometimes a kind of suspicion shades her features, when turned towards the stranger knight.

When admitted at the gates, he said he was come in search of adventures: seeing the castle on his way, he advanced for refreshment. During the last meal of the evening, some of the company made mention of the haunted apartments. The Duke laughed at the idea, and declared he had long ridiculed the whole story.—He whom you call Count Richard affirmed the same; and with a voice of stifled emotion, said it was merely raised by idle and impertinent people, who knew not wherefore that wing was uninhabited: but that the fools gave way to every impulse of fear and superstition.

This occasioned much debate on the subject of ghosts; and the haunted wing was several times rementioned; when at last Brunchilda, with a countenance of rage and often fear (alternately from pale to red, and from red to pale) requested so ridiculous a conversation might have an end. Again the Count, her brother, joined her in essaying to change the subject; and he seemed considerably more angry at it than his sister. It was remarked by the English knight, Sir Raymond Fitz-Henry, but remarked in silence; neither was the confusion of Hubert (for I call him by no other name) or the anger of Brunchilda lost on the stranger. Some person present, who seemed more actuated by the spirit of tormenting than curiosity, and who had made the same observations which the two knights had done, determined to prevent the closing of that discourse. — "Surely," said he, "murders have been there committed!"

'And who has authorized you,' imperiously, demanded Brunchilda, 'to fancy the castle of my ancestors has been stained with blood?'

'I do not fancy it, Madam,' said the person, with a smile half apologetic, half sarcastic; 'but the troubled spirits of the departed do not walk there for nothing!'

"Ridiculous idea!" cried Brunchilda; "weak supposition!"

'May I enquire,' said the teizer, turning to the Duke, 'why those apartments were shut up, and rendered totally useless by all persons being excluded from them?'

Brunchilda, whose eyes now sparkled with rage, waited not for Albert's answer, but replied, "We want them not; we have sufficient room without entering those damp and dreary places."

The curiosity of Grimoald seemed now awakened; and as he said at his first entrance, he was come in search of adventures, he thought there was no impropriety in asking permission to sleep in those apartments in preference to any others.—He added, 'My returning safe in the morning from them, will convince both your attendants and your vassals that the ghosts only walk in the regions of their imagination. Those ideas then, which your lady (perhaps justly) calls so ridiculous, will be for ever banished; and the poor rats and owls (for such I in general believe ghosts to be) suffered to possess their habitation in tranquillity and peace.'

"Sir knight," replied Brunchilda, "you have already rooms allotted you in the habitable part of the building; and as they are such as we ever give to those we treat with respect and hospitality, should they not be what are satisfactory to you, either this night or to-morrow you may take your departure:—seek through the other courts of France, and discover if they are better. Perhaps you will, after your search, have reason to avow their grandeur consists of ineffectual trials to affect that magnificence which we really and easily support."

She hoped, by giving it this turn, she should effect her purpose of quieting the querists: however, feeling herself much agitated, and fearing to be discovered, she arose from the table and retired, as quickly did her brother. Their departure occasioned the breaking up of the company; and each retired to rest, except Albert, Sir Raymond, and Grimoald the Avenger.

'I fear (said Grimoald, when they were gone) my questions concerning the castle have offended the lady.'

"They seem so to have done," replied the Duke; "yet I really know not why they should.—Still I observe, whenever the subject is mentioned she always prevents its being carried on; which I suppose arises from her dislike to such folly.—Indeed she always declares that to be the reason."

'Surely,' said Grimoald, 'my having remained in them this night, would have prevented her being troubled with such tales in future.'

"I think so myself," said the Duke; "but my lady always strenuously opposes every thing of the kind, though it has often been proposed. I would have permitted it myself, but ladies, you know, seldom admire opposition, unless it is their own parts."

'How long have they been disused?' asked Raymond. — "I know not exactly," said Albert; "but they were so long before I became master of this castle; which I did on my marriage with Brunchilda, to whose father it belonged. We have more room than we ever want already; and I never thought it material either to open them, or enquire wherefore they were shut up."

Perhaps then you are uninformed of the reports which have been long and widely spread, injurious to your own and your lady's honour?

I have often heard that the peasantry thought them haunted, and of the plebeian opinions of former bloody deeds; but have ever treated them as idle rumours deserve; besides, little blame can surely attach to me when those places were uninhabited before the death of the prince who last possessed it. — Grimoald replied, 'Although hitherto a stranger to you and your lady, I am not so to the popular legends of your castle, some of which have reached to distant provinces. One of the storms of this evening obliged me to seek shelter for myself and palfrey in one of the cottages belonging to the peasantry surrounding the castle: I had seen the towers rising above the trees, and having remarked the peculiar beauty of its appearance, I asked to whom it belonged. They informed me that Duke Albert was the owner. On hearing your name, I recollected to have heard of Duke Albert's haunted habitation; but this I did not notice to them, being curious to know what any of them would say, unassisted by my recital of foreign stories on the subject. Further:—I wished to know

24

whether what I had heard concerning the popular opinions of these domains was true.'

The Duke here interrupted Grimoald. "What then, you really do believe in apparitions?"

'No, certainly not: that could not be deduced from what I have said. Indeed I believe you have heard me give it as an opinion, that they were in general owls or rats. At the same time I declare to you, I never yet found the story of a ghost gain so much belief, and so long influence the minds of the people, attended with the circumstances this is, that had not some knavery for its support. I therefore never hear of any thing of the kind without a determination not to relinquish my search till I have made an entire discovery of the whole affair. Under the influence of this opinion, I asked them if there was any thing in particular in the neighbourhood to see? Were there any ghosts which gave them trouble? or, Were there any injuries which wanted discovery and redressing?—At this, one of the peasants stared for some time at me, and then sat down and laughed a long while. I was much amused to observe his mirth; but very unable to account for it. When he had expended his breath and merriment sufficiently to give me a chance of an answer, I asked him the reason of his risibility.—Oh Lord, Sir, to think what a mortal great man you take yourself for!—Is there any thing curious to see? any ghosts to drive out? or any injury to redress?—Mercy on us!—Why now, pray Sir, supposing I was to tell you the Duke had a she-devil locked in a box in the northern wing, and would let nobody see it on pain of death, would you go and try?—No, my friend, I replied; I should not think her worth going after, especially on pain of death.—Why, said the man, I know many a fool of a knight that would do so, merely because it was hard to be done, though it had no other merit than its difficulty. But what if I were to say there were as many ghosts as windows in the northern wing?—Why, my friend, as I never yet was hurt by a ghost, though I have attacked a large number, I should not care if there were as many ghosts as leaves upon the trees which surround the castle.—'No doubt on't, Sir, for I fancy you would find it hard to see any leaves on the trees, since these cold winds and sharp frosts have carried them all away. But, Sir, the people here all declare they have seen the goblins at every window and tower of the castle. Now I have been round a hundred times, dark and dusk, light and bright, and never saw a ghost yet. As for injuries, you must be a god to redress them, for of late there is not a peasant but what has suffered by the horrible and uncommon oppression of the Duke and his Brunchilda.— Devil take 'em, say I.'

"I am infinitely obliged," said Albert, "both for his account of my oppression, and his reward at the end of it. I cannot guess wherefore he thus blackens my character.—I thought my vassals were happy and contented; it has ever been my study to render them so:—but continue, I request you."

As soon as this man had done speaking, a young woman addressed him:—I am sure it is very strange you could never see any ghosts when so many other people see them every night, and all the Duke's servants believe them!—And of whom do you believe them to be the ghosts?—Oh dear, if I was to say, and the Lady

Brunchilda was to hear it, we should be all killed, and our spirits sent to live with the others in the castle.

'Oh, fear not. Should the reports be false, she can never be angry at them, as they must be too ridiculous to gain any credit.'

'Ah, Sir, there is but one good person in the castle, and that is the Lady Hildegarde; she never can be the daughter of two such sad tyrants, because she is so good to us:—and her mother hates her so!—But, Sir, they say that when the Lady Gunilda (who was mother to our present lady) was alive, that all of a sudden a Count Richard and his wife and servants were all missing; and before that, a little son of her husband's first wife was gone too: so the Lady Gunilda and her son said he had been a very bad man.'

"Who had been a very bad man?"

'Why, Sir, the Count Richard: and that when he thought his bad ways were found out, he run away one night (but nobody believes it) because, soon after he went, the lady ordered all that side of the castle to be shut up, because such strange voices and noises were heard there. And then her son, who used to be called the Count Hubert, had all his estates and money, and took the title of Count Richard; and gave orders if any one dared to mention the bad Count, or call him (that is Hubert, Sir) or, I say, call him Hubert, and not call him Richard, they should die for it!—'

Could not the people have complained to the king?—Oh they would have got no good by that; for none of our great lords in France mind the king now:— and they have a vast deal more power over us poor vas- sals than the king has: they be sad tyrants. Why, Sir,

27

they said the Lady Brunchilda's mother had made away with them!

Thus did the damsel chatter and comment, until the storm being over, I remounted my horse, and advanced towards the castle:—and I wish I had your permission, unknown to your Lady, to search these mysterious apartments.

The Duke, who had sat silent and gloomy during the remainder of the discourse, now broke silence.—My friend, said he, the night is too far advanced to admit of our searching those apartments now, because we shall be obliged to spend so much time in opening the great doors which lead to them; but so great an effect has the relation made on me, of the people's opinions, and so much have I been surprised at the confusion and anger of my lady, that if you will grant me your company and assistance to-morrow night, I will put an end to this unpleasant affair. I wish not to have my intentions known to Brunchilda: I will therefore feign indisposition, that we may all retire early; but when the castle is quiet, and there is no fear of interruption, I will call you from your chambers, and we will proceed to the rooms.

They easily consented to the proposal of the Duke; and soon after this they retired for repose.

And how could you gain this intelligence? asked Jacquemar.—Inquisitive animal, did I not forbid thee to enquire? replied the old man.

Early that evening Grodern expressed a sense of great fatigue, pleaded his age, and said he was indisposed: he requested their leave to retire, and begged he might not be disturbed. On this he departed to the cell

28

which was appointed for him, leaving Jacquemar much amazed at his intelligence, and the means by which he could obtain it. Having heard Grodern complain much of a severe indisposition, Jacquemar arose in the middle of the night, and, going to his cell, softly opened the door: but softly as it was done, it awakened Grodern, who angrily demanded what he wanted.—Jacquemar replied, fearing he might be worse in the night, he had only come to see if his friend wanted any thing, and if he reposed well.—Seeming only half satisfied, Grodern bid him return, and never again attempt to disturb him.

Next morning they were all summoned by the abbess to matins, and afterwards they met to take some refreshment. Grodern said he was much benefitted by the rest he had taken, and declared himself well. I had been up some time, said he, when we were called to matins.

Then perhaps, said Jacquemar, smiling, you can tell more of the haunted rooms?

You must fancy my messengers are then very swift, to come all the way from the castle sufficiently early to deliver me any account of them. I can tell you, however, that your favourite Alwin will be here; therefore when Edward comes, remember Alwin. But we must not now stay for parley; let us procure our disguises.

Soon were Jacquemar and Edgar equipped like monks; and Grodern left them, as he said, to disguise himself. No person arrived at the convent all day; and they began to doubt the veracity of their old intelligencer. The convent was near the castle; but being divided from it by a river (which kept winding on very far before it was overarched by a bridge) the foot or horse-road was many miles round.

Jacquemar, having for that day lost his consolatory friend, fell again into his almost unmanly sorrows: and now the good abbess exerted her warmest efforts to soothe and cheer him. In her whole conduct was conspicuous that true benevolence and charity which are ever remarkable in the lives of those who practise what they preach, and whose doctrine is the effort of belief, not of assent, or compliance with established form or popular opinion, merely because it is such. This convent was more remarkable for the spirit of Christianity than the *furor* of devotion: it was rather the asylum of the unfortunate than the retreat of enthusiasts: it was of an order similar to the Grey Sisters, whose whole time is spent in offices of charity.

They had retained their disguises all the remainder of the day, and were at night sitting round a cheerful fire, talking of the small necessity there appeared to be of keeping them any longer; when they were suddenly alarmed by a loud and impatient knocking at the exterior gates of the convent. Ere the abbess would allow the gates to be opened, she concealed the children in a closet, whose door was perfectly imperceptible to all who were unacquainted with it. She then suffered the gates to be unlocked. A party from the castle immediately rushed in, and demanded further entrance. This was denied them until they showed an order from Duke Albert to have the refugees given up, or, on refusal, a command to search the convent for them. The abbess in vain expostulated with them: she urged to them the indelicacy of their proceedings, and the impropriety of their suffering a rude band to range the convent and interrupt her nuns.—But the wind would have been as passive had she forbid its blasts to howl around her. By dint of much entreaty she gained permission to conduct her flock into one large room, which had been first searched, and lock them in to secure them from wanton insult. This having been done, the convent was entirely passed over by Brunchilda's emissaries: but no person after whom they had made enquiry was discovered, until, seeing the two monks, Edward demanded from whence they came.

Cannot you discover that their habit is of the neighbouring monastry? did the abbess reply.

And what are their names?

The abbess hesitated. They had forgotten to name them.

Speak, madam, this instant, said Edward, with the countenance of suspicion and the voice of anger.

"Father Everard, and Father Anselm."

'Rather, madam, say villain Jacquemar and rascal Edgar. But pray, where is Father Grodern?'

The abbess was terrified, but replied he was not within her convent-walls.

'And pray, madam, how came these holy men within your convent-walls? were they admitted to protect your nuns? Doubtless, the young Edgar is a proper guard. Perhaps they mean to take the veil?'

The abbess, whose conduct and whose management of her vestals was such as was unspotted, only answered with a smile of dignity and contempt.

Madam, I shall find a way to make you answer and repent your scorn. I demand who are they? — Alas! said the abbess, trembling for the fate of her guests, alas! as poor unfortunate travellers, they came to seek my protection, and besought me to grant them in my convent an asylum for a few days, from the persecution of their enemies, and during the inclemency of the weather. One brought his wife in very ill, and has since had the misfortune to lose her; and I could not be so cruel as to turn them out again without first trying to restore the unfortunate and mournful husband to peace and cheerfulness.

On your life, madam, declare where the traitor Grodern is concealed!—This uttered, Edward, at the same time, drew a dagger and presented it to her heart!

Stay Sir, said she, again resuming her dignity, and a look which awed the insolent:—Stay Sir,—the sacred character I bear must prevent your assassination of me:—and by all the terrors of the holy church which shall be denounced on you and your employers, I charge you hold. You have already violated the honour of this sacred place: you have dared to search the convent: you have not found the chief object of your search: the others claim my protection:—I give it, and I demand your immediate absence.

Edward drew back, conscious he had not received orders to proceed thus far; and dreading the wrath of the holy father to whom the abbess might appeal, and whose mandate Albert would obey, notwithstanding all that Grodern had affirmed to Jacquemar, still he continued to demand the surrender of the two men.—The abbess still refused to give consent: and Edward dared not to seize them, because they were under the protection of the church. Their defendress declared they should remain unmolested with her until some deeds of guilt were proved against them.—I will not, said she, betray the confidence they have placed in me; neither dare you to violate the trust. I charge you then, under pain of the severest anathemas from Italy, to leave them undisturbed.

Intimidated by her firmness, Edward withdrew, muttering curses, and vowing revenge.

The band being departed, the nuns were conducted back to their cells, and the party again surrounded the fire. Grodern was still away: neither did they see any thing more of him that night: much did his absence surprize them; and many conjectures did they form: but as neither surprize or conjecture could bring them back, they retired to rest without him.

The next morning he joined them at breakfast. The curious Jacquemar so overwhelmed him with enquiries, and was so importunate for an answer, that he scarcely permitted him to make a repast. Having at last finished, Grodern told him he had been in safety, and was able to give nearly all the information he wished. I shall continue, said he, from where I yesterday concluded, concerning the haunted apartments; for, should I at first answer your other queries, you will not become sufficiently calm and silent to listen to the reply I should make to the last.

After supper the Duke, as was agreed on, complained of fatigue, and said he was not sufficiently well to sit up longer. Brunchilda seemed pleased at this declaration; but he knew not wherefore: she soon departed, as did the rest of the company. The two knights imagined the weariness of the Duke proceeded merely from design, and was as feigned as he had said it should be: each of them therefore retired to his chamber, where they anxiously waited, every minute expecting the promised summons, but in vain; Duke Albert never came. Fatigued at length, and sick of waiting, they composed themselves to rest, each suspecting the Duke had some reason for the breaking of his word; and this suspicion made Grimoald more determined than ever to search to the bottom of a mystery which began, in his opinion, to have a very bad appearance.

Little blame could attach to the Duke in this affair. Finding himself in reality as much fatigued as he said, and uncommonly heavy, he threw himself on his couch, merely to rest until the inhabitants of the castle were hushed; but a deep sleep overtook him, and when he awaked, found it was late in the morning, and that he was drest and in his own chamber as over-night. In a few minutes the natural surprise which attended his first waking (and ere his ideas and memory became unconfused) left him on his recollecting the excessive sleepyness he had felt the night before; and which lately had not become uncommon to him. The neglect he had been guilty of, and the disappointment he had in consequence occasioned the knights, made him appear greatly confused when he first beheld Grimoald and Sir Raymond Fitz-Henry; conscious they would think the affront great, and have reason to suspect that he deserved the popular opinion. He was justified in this idea by the gravity with which they received his compliments of the morning: and both hastily addressing him, informed him they intended taking their leave of the castle that same day. This they had both previously agreed on: they had also determined to remain in the neighbourhood until they could contrive some method of discovering the truth, and to declare their unravelling the mystery.

After much intreaty and many avowals of sincerity; after having produced witnesses from amongst his own servants of the frequency of this unaccountable drowsiness, he with much trouble prevailed on them to stay yet another night beneath his roof: in which they should explore the haunted chambers.

Gloomy and morose was the lady of Duke Albert all the preceding day; for he had often changed his mind during the time. He disliked the measure of searching the convent, and thought it profane; but at length, by importunity she gained his final consent; and her ill-mannered attendants, as you are a witness of, put her designs in execution. When she found that you were discovered and not brought back by her emissaries, her rage was unbounded; and she vowed when alone with her beloved paramour Edward, she would be amply revenged on the abbess for the protection she had afforded you—Chiefly was she incensed that I was missing.

Jacquemar could not here restrain his love of questioning; but requested to know what had made Brunchilda so much the enemy of so apparently insignificant an old man.

In some part I can reply to your queries. Viewing the extreme beauty and gracefulness of Edgar, she wished him to become one of her chief domestics: often she sent to me for him. At first I treated her messengers with great coolness and contempt; but at least she desired he might become a gardener to the castle. In this situation I imagined him more safe from her wiles than were he in any other. I therefore suffered him to go; but he speedily found this place subjected him more to her company than that of a servant in the castle would have done. Under pretences of walking and being fond of plants, she would go where Edgar was working: she would call him from his labour to attend to her whims. The folly she showed in her distribution, with her inattention to soil or season, proved it was neither fondness for or knowledge of agriculture which had made her attempt any alterations. Edgar at first would remonstrate with her on the want of skill she showed: this seemed to please her; and she would endeavour to draw on long conversations. In a short time he began to remark, that she paid him an uncommon attention, and that her whole carriage towards him savoured more of love than of decorum. Edgar had even a bad opinion of the lady: he could witness the cruelty of her treatment of Hildegarde: he could observe the strong contrast in the behaviour of these females; and as his admiration of the one increased, his disgust towards the other heightened.

Brunchilda gave him hints, which could not be but understood; but he feigned ignorance. This increased the passion of the lady; and she spoke at length in such terms, that he could no longer pretend to misunderstand her. Knowing that, in females, disappointed passion often turns to the most inveterate hatred, he thought it best to quit her service before it became too late: he therefore left her, and returned home.

Soon after, as he was passing through the forest, he there beheld one of her domestics (indeed I may inform you it was the identical Edward to whom we are now so much obliged) quarrelling with a poor vassal of the Duke Albert; and not contented with abusing the man, proceeded to beat him with the greatest brutality; which the age and weakness of the other prevented him from resisting. Edgar flew to his assistance, and rescued him from the cruelty of Edward. This was repeated to Brunchilda, with every aggravation which falsehood could invent; since which she has often essayed to bring us to the castle; but in vain: we know her disappointed pride and the malice of her parasite would be our immediate ruin. Our present baffling of her plans has made her determine to spare no pains to accomplish our overthrow. Speaking of me last night, said she, "there lurks in the countenance of that old traitor some deep and hidden purpose; his eye never meets mine with the bashful timidity of the humble peasant, but with the half concealed determination and angry ferocity of the injured equal; however, to-morrow shall give to my revenge himself and son. Neither shall his friend, his Jacquemar, escape; and we will sit in judgment within the abbey-walls; and do you, my faithful Edward, prepare the men this night to swear with caution.—"Where are those two men who seized on Dunisleda?"

'Ready at hand for orders, answered Edward.'

"At night, then, when the Duke is retired, bring them to me: and mind,—when at supper Albert calls for the cup, infuse, as thou hast often done, this sleeping potion. This, my dear Edward, has often prevented him from disturbing our plans by his presence; and this shall again do so."

Edward then saluted the wife of his master, and retired to perform her orders. Brunchilda joined the party; and having informed the Duke of their discovery, obtained his permission to sit in judgment on the next day. Knowing how trivial in general were the causes of her complaint, he did not hesitate; his mercy made him hope the unfortunate men would be found innocent. At the same time, knowing how much her malevolent disposition would generally make her determined to misconstrue the matter, he resolved to attend the examination, accompanied by the two knights.

At supper, Edward infused the potion; but the Duke drank not thereof: he suspected something was wrong, and determined to be very wary: he well knew another sleeping accident would ruin him for ever in the opinion of his guests. To this must be attributed his absence of the former nights, and that heaviness he had so often complained of. His not drinking it was observed by Edward, by Brunchilda, and her brother; the latter of whom held the Duke in detestation. Perhaps you have never beheld this man: I will therefore describe him to you, as, in my opinion, his person in some measure is strongly marked with his character:—His figure is tall, and size gigantic; his complexion of the darkest hue: thick and sable eye-brows hung low over his fierce and hawk-like eyes; he wears his beard short and bushy; but it nearly covers the lower part of his face: the stile of his dress adds to the ferocity of his appearance; and his manners (except constrained) are as ungentle as his mind is dark. Long has he despised the Duke for the sincerity of his disposition; for that he calls meanness. Often has Albert given his pardon to the simple offenders arraigned by his lady: and to a soul which harbours nothing but revenge, forgiveness is a crime. Long has he envied the Duke his possessions; part of which Brunchilda has promised shall belong to him upon her husband's death. He had been informed by his sister that the sleeping draught was to be given him that night; and he therefore, on finding the Duke abstain from drinking of the cup, thought they were suspected. In the morning a dispute had taken place between Hubert and the Duke; in which the latter had not spoken much to the praise or satisfaction of the Earl, who retired from his presence angry and revengeful. The whole day had been passed in ruminating on the affront he had received. His pride inflamed him to so violent a degree, that he determined to murder Albert that night when the draught had hushed him in the arms of sleep; but when he found the first had not been taken, he determined to postpone the second. He was invited to accompany his sister to the trial on the ensuing day, but refused, having resolved to remain at the castle and plot the evening's assassination. When Albert again complained of being ill and weary, each of the traitors believed he really was so, and imputed it to the effects of the last night's potion; which, they imagined, were not yet entirely evaporated: He was therefore suffered to retire without further remark or demur, more especially as the early dissolving of the party suited the scheme of the lady.

When all seemed quiet, the Duke, now punctual to his promise, called upon the knights; and both in complete armour were ready to attend him. They immediately proceeded to the haunted wing, which was in part, at least such as was more modern, built exactly to answer its opposite one: the only difference consisted in some heavy architecture, constructed by the Goths at the time they over-run that part of France in which were the territories of Duke Albert: all the other parts had been added to it by the ancestors of Brunchilda's father-in-law, the husband of Gunilda. With great difficulty they unclosed the folding doors, which from a court in the center of the castle, opened upon a passage which led into it. Scarcely would they turn upon their hinges, on account of the rust which had thickened around them. Still were the adventurers much surprised to find them but slightly fastened up; but they imputed it to the haste in which some fear had caused Gunilda to desert that wing (for that there was some evil deed or cause for fear they now all began to fancy) and to the little curiosity servants in those days in general feel to encounter ghosts: beings they readily believed the existence of, and of whom they most strenuously wished to avoid the sight.

Damp, musty, and unwholesome vapours issued from every room; in most of which they found the furniture remaining as if people had but a minute before ceased to use them: some placed by the ashes of fires which seemed just decayed; some placed at tables on which the vessels yet remained; but all covered with the accumulated dust of distant times. In some rooms the ravages of time, added to the weakening of neglect, had brought the roofing to decay; the rains had entered, and the damp had clothed the walls with its verdant mantle;

whilst all the moveables were covered with the grey spotting mildew; and any thing which arose from the labours of the loom, fell to pieces on removal. Here the worm worked its winding cloisters, and there the spider spread her mazy dwelling; devastation and decay had passed through each apartment. They continued to go through all the lower suite of rooms without meeting ghost or goblin, or any thing worth further notice, until coming to a large room, they beheld a table surrounded by seats, and spread with viands all dusty, and of ancient date. Some were decayed in the dishes, and others dried and mouldy: as to their nature and sort, time had made that impossible to guess; but it appeared as if people had arisen from a splendid feast, where the rites of Bacchus had not been neglected; or rather let me say, were meant to be celebrated; for the vessels remained wherein the liquor had dried up, or become unfit for use.

What a waste of furniture and provision is there here! exclaimed Sir Raymond; and by what could all this have been occasioned?

Occasioned! reiterated Grimoald: it betrays the haste of guilt and sudden impulses of fear. These apartments could not have been thus abandoned and secured from entry for trifles, or for nothing.

Albert felt and acknowledged the justice of his speech; but further could only feel surprized and look concerned. Although, on account of the time elapsed, no suspicion of his having acted in these deeds could attach to him, yet he well knew it might with reason be suspected that he had known and concealed the guilt.

Having contemplated a while the scene before them, Grimoald said angrily, Let us proceed: I question, Duke

41

Albert, if we shall not find here that which will terminate thy rule and power over these domains!

The Duke and Raymond asked an explanation.

Time, answered the Avenger, which shall uncover my shield, shall unfold these deeds; shall prove thou art no longer lord or owner here: Another comes armed with the sword of vengeance and the power of right: till then thou reignest.

They could not persuade him to say more. Raymond was surprized, and Albert angry; but neither surprize or anger had any effect on Grimoald, who, leaving the chamber, led to the way up stairs. Having ascended a long flight, they passed through several rooms; where nothing attracted their attention, and of which they left every door open as they proceeded, that they the more easily might discover through which they had been. They everywhere, as below, saw furniture remaining.

This ghost-hunting is very unprofitable, said Raymond. We may as well go into the remaining chambers, said Albert.

True, added Grimoald; and there are others remaining, through which we have not yet been.

Thus saying, he attempted to open the door of a room they had just arrived at, but found resistance. Examining for the cause, he discovered it was locked on the out-side; but no key remained whereby he could open it. The Duke told him he was determined to have it opened before he left that wing; and they went in search of some instruments by which they could effect this purpose. Shortly they procured an iron implement which had been used for the fires; and, returning with it, Albert himself forced the door open. Here every thing seemed as in other places, until turning towards a couch, the Duke touching some clothes which covered it, observed how much good might have been done by distributing amongst the poor labourers of the forest the profusion of articles which he now beheld spoiled and rotting.

Disturb not the ashes of the departed!—exclaimed a hollow voice from the bed.

Sir Raymond advanced and drew his sword, and attempted to look under the clothes.

Again a voice exclaimed, Destroy not the repose of the dead!

What villain lurks there? furiously cried Grimoald, and rushed forward immediately with the light, which he had carried all the way. A groan assailed his ear:—he tore off the coverings in a rage;—something turned in the bed; he advanced the light, saying, Speak, miscreant, and explain wherefore you are here!—holding the light close to it, he expected to behold some trembling imposture, or some hardened villain; but the hollow skull and dry bones of a skeleton met his eye. He started with the suddenness of the surprize, and, starting, dropped the lamp. In vain they attempted to restore the light; the last spark soon expired, and they were left in total darkness. Each drew his sword, but knew not whither they should turn; for one minute the cold feet of fear were felt creeping over their bodies, and their hearts beat quick.

Whither shall we go now? asked the Duke. We will open the windows, said the impetuous Grimoald, in a rude tone; the star-light may direct us.

We will thank you to find them first, replied the milder Englishman.

After a few minutes they discovered where they were; Grimoald laid his hand upon an iron bar which crossed one of them, and was attempting to loosen it, when the hand of the skeleton fastened upon his arm, and a stern voice bid him quit the chambers, saying also, that the mysteries of those places were not for his discovery.—He again started, and in the action of receding, he found the hand seem to unfasten from something, and fall upon the ground.

Not knowing what could be the cause of this, and ignorant of how many they might have to contend with, Raymond proposed retiring. We are in the dark, said he, and may in vain try to defend ourselves from enemies we cannot see.

True, said a voice which sounded near him; and to him who stays 'tis death. Let those who would be safe, follow yonder light.

Turning round, they saw at a great distance a small light illuminate the walls of some chambers: they advanced towards it, but could see no person, because it was kept at so wide a distance as only to suffer them to behold the places through which it passed. It led them down some stairs, which they imagined were the same they had ascended by; after which it passed on through some rooms and a passage, and rested at the end. They then heard a great noise, like the letting down of heavy chains; and entering the passage, they viewed the light shine on some folding doors.—Depart through those doors, said the voice behind them.—They turned, to see from whence it came; but all being utter darkness, they perceived nothing: they therefore went up to the doors, and the light which had turned up another passage now disappeared. They opened them, as they were unfastened, and found themselves in the open air. The doors immediately closed upon them.—We are now again within the court, said the Duke: but they speedily discovered they were deceived; they walked forward, but found their passage interrupted by weeds, briars, and broken stones; neither did the stars give the light which Grimoald promised, as a cloudy sky had obscured them. Sometimes the ground was damp and swampy. — We cannot proceed, said Raymond; the darkness of the night prevents our finding the way, and we may get into the river which flows at the back of the castle; whither I suspect we are now come. So saying, he turned to go back, and beheld a light on high, nearly, as he could judge, on the turrets of the castle. — There is our perfidious director, said Raymond.

"Be polite, and do not call names, English knight. Leave that to great Grimoald," said a voice from above them.

'Descend, foul fiend, and take us from this gloom,' holla'd Grimoald.—

"Your epithets are not encouraging," replied the voice.

'Damnation!' exclaimed Grimoald; 'are we to be made the objects of a villain's trifling!'

"You are too warm: the river is near, jump in and cool yourself."

'If you do not come down, by hell and all its furies, you shall repent.'

"Come up, and make me, great Grimoald the Avenger! Come, and hunt the owls and rats."

Grimoald was conscious he could not, therefore raved the more.

"Be tamer. Good night, ghost-hunter!" said the teizing goblin.—

Grimoald swore in vain: the cold made it an unpleasant situation for the Duke and Raymond; and although they were in the same situation as the Avenger, yet they could not help heartily laughing at his anger, and threatening the ghost. This did not serve to appease him; for he began more loudly to rail.—'If I could catch the rascally dog, I would wring his neck off,' said he.

"Good night," said the voice, close to him.

Grimoald dashed his weapon around on all sides, aiming at the ghost. Scarcely could his companions escape his fury, until, pacing round in great anger, he sunk in a swamp! He cried out to them for assistance; but as he kept struggling, and still hewing the air, they chose not to venture near. His action only made him sink the deeper.

'This ghost-hunting is a pleasant affair,' said Raymond; 'and, were it not for our participation of it, I should like to see a little of it every night.'

For some time the enraged Avenger would not consent to be quiet: they therefore let him stick a little, meanwhile some voices sung near him,

> Now to the goddess of the night
> We'll consecrate this angry wight;
> And when he's roasted red with ire,

> Hence we'll tear him,
> Then we'll bear him
> Down to our Satanic sire!

A dismal yelling succeeded, and Grimoald the Avenger promised to be very pacific as well as quiet, if the Duke and knight would extricate him from the swamp. This they did, being nearly as much surprized as himself at the adventures of the evening, but much more diverted. As soon as he was released, the voices again sung.

> Glorious Grimoald, deign to say,
> Wilt thou in the castle stay,
> Hunt the ghosts, or run away?
> When other beings love to sleep,
> Wilt thou in thy chamber keep,
> Or come here at ghosts to peep?
> Son of Anasleda, say,
> If to hell thou'lt wing the way?
> Speak! we can no longer stay.

'On my word,' said Raymond, 'these are the merriest devils I ever met with: we have none such in England.'

Albert, who though he might for a moment when surprize had suspended consideration, experience the first attacks of fear, had in the main too much good sense to believe in goblins: all the superstition of the age could not convince him there were any such beings; he was therefore not at all sorry at the curious adventure of Grimoald, whose conduct had been far from polite. He suspected it was some trick of the inhabitants of the castle, who had overheard their intention of visiting these rooms.

Grimoald began to upbraid the Duke for the whole of it, taxing him with being the contriver. This, said Albert, is easily contradicted: for, had not your fears made you drop the lamp, we should have seen our way safely out of the castle. All we have now to do is to rest in peace, until the morning shews us how we may escape.

The next morning found all the three adventurers swearing, shivering, grumbling, and laughing: and the light convinced them it was as Raymond suspected; they were at the back of the castle, but they in vain sought for the folding doors through which they had been brought thither; nothing of the kind appeared. At this Raymond laughed more than ever, and requested earnestly that the Duke would send Grimoald to hunt ghosts again the ensuing night. They found the place in which the Avenger had stuck was a muddy ditch which went round part of the old buildings, and communicated with the river.

As soon as possible they re-entered the castle, unseen by any one but the old porter, who much wondered to see them on the out-side; but was commanded by the Duke to say nothing of it.

Now then, having no further intelligence to give you, I must retire; ere long Albert will be here:—have courage, and shew your innocence by your regular and connected answers to all the questions they may chuse to put to you; but especially speak slow, that you may recollect all you have answered to their first enquiries;

so that should you be asked the same question over again, you may be able to give the same answer. Let truth rule every word; no double questioning then can ever injure.

This said, Grodern departed; and soon after the arrival of Duke Albert, Brunchilda and their train were announced. Albert demanded that the nave of the convent-church should be given to them, to try the accused party in. He contended, that a judgment upon life or death was a business too solemn to profane that place: It was a matter in which every man concerned should appeal to Heaven, and on the mercy of God fix his reliance: God alone, said he, can prove who is innocent or guilty; therefore no place can be more proper than his dwelling, and in his presence.

They assembled in the nave; then were led forth Jacquemar and Edgar, the wife of Grodern, and the young children. "And are these innocents included in the crime?" asked Albert, sighing.

Yes, yes, said Brunchilda, all of the guilty race.— Take them hence, said the Duke, they surely must be free.—A smile irradiated the sorrowful countenance of Jacquemar at the release of his children; and a tear trembled in each eye as he fell on his knees to thank his master.

Rise, young man, said Albert, I am come hither to do justice; your children could not be guilty; or even had they dipped their hands in the blood of Conrad, yet they must be ignorant of their crime. He only can be called an offender against the laws, who knows what those laws are against which he has offended.

Indeed then, most noble prince, replied the simple Jacquemar, I knew not it was a crime when I killed Conrad.

"He is guilty, he is guilty," joyfully exclaimed Brunchilda; "hear himself acknowledge it."

The Duke made no reply: he was so much surprised by the great simplicity of the man, that he knew not what answer to make.

Sir Raymond, fearing it would pass off in this manner, arose, and addressing Albert, said he hoped it was not the law in those territories to pass sentence on a man from his own accusation, before he had given in his defence.

He has said he is guilty, said Brunchilda, and what want we more?

His reasons for having been so, madam.

Albert turning to Brunchilda, with a more severe countenance than was usual, said, Madam, I came here to do justice, not to feed revenge; and I command silence.—Where is Grodern?

The abbess answered the Duke, that she actually knew not. Unusual as it was for ladies of her situation to mix with knights and the gay trains of courts, she also was obliged to be present by the express order of Albert, whom she could not disobey.

And now the accusers of the party being called for, Edward and two men came forward, saying they were ready. Edward spoke for them: He declared that Jacquemar, Grodern, and his son, accompanied by Dunisleda, were returning to their cottages, when they overtook two men belonging to the household of the Duke, but in the particular service of Brunchilda: that

Dunisleda separated from the party, and joined the two men, trying by her arts and wanton allurements to draw them home: that they resented her behaviour, and refused to accompany her.

Oh God! cried Jacquemar, clasping his hands, what cruel falsehoods!

Silence, said the Duke, or we shall think you guilty.—

I cannot be silent! indeed I cannot!—my poor Dunisleda is gone! she is dead! she died all by their cruelty! and now they tell such lies!—

Young man, when your accuser has said all he can against you, you will be allowed to say all you can against him: but if we have any more interruptions, we will directly condemn you.

The accuser continued:—

The others came up and attempted to murder them at the same time, bidding them deliver up all they had about them; declaring they knew they had money; that he (the accuser) came up, and being armed, rescued them: that the accused then fled: that they in their flight met and murdered Conrad, the servant of Brunchilda, and had murdered, robbed, and buried him near the convent.

To this the two men then swore also.

Have you any more to say? asked Albert. He was answered, No.

Jacquemar was then suffered to give his defence; which having done, the Duke arose, and said he should now give his judgment:—That the tale of the accused seemed more probable than that of the accuser; and he could not call them guilty: but that it should rest upon the opinion of three of the oldest men present. Two of these declared them innocent; but the third desired that the accused should be searched, to discover if they had any thing which had belonged to Conrad about them.

Brunchilda now desired to speak.

I had given, said she, to Conrad that morning a small bag of money and a cross of jewels to carry to the abbey of ———: neither of which were found on the body; because, along with his clothes, these murderers had taken the cross and bag.

Jacquemar, happy to find his fate depend upon what he thought was sure to prove his innocence, gladly called upon them to come and search him:—he was searched; but neither money nor jewels had the poor cottager.

The son of Grodern was next to be examined.

Most noble Duke, said Edgar, save yourself the time and trouble; pronounce us innocent, for neither money nor jewels have I seen, though it was I who buried the body of Conrad.

They are surely innocent, said the Duke.—Let them be searched, said the lady. The son was searched; and in a fold of his garment was discovered a cross of jewels!— His ancient mother fainted!—Jacquemar stood aghast in silent agony.—The Duke sighed deeply!

Brunchilda smiled the smile of malice high trium-phant; and the son of Grodern hung his head low, as if in confusion.—For a while all were silent: some watching the emotions of others—some buried in their own, until Edward stepped forward, demanding of the Duke if he wished for any other proof to find the miscreants guilty?—if this would not convince him, let him add the flight of Grodern, who, in all probability, had carried the money with him.

The Duke neither regarded him nor spoke: sorrow oppressed his heart; and he mourned for the depravity of a fellow-creature.

Now, hapless Edgar, what shall save thee from the malice of thy accuser? where shalt thou find a shelter from the overwhelming torrent? Edgar, there is a Being who formed the poor and formed the mighty: he who guards the life of the human being, protects the emmet also!

Sir Raymond now arose, and again requested leave to interfere.

Brunchilda frowned upon him; for Brunchilda hated Raymond. She requested no strangers might have permission to interfere in her concerns.

Madam, replied Raymond, in a matter merely concerning yourself, perhaps it would be improper to interfere; but when the lives of several of our fellow-creatures depend upon the single evidence of a favourite, or of people probably suborned by him, it is then time for every one to examine, and, if possible, preserve from death the unfortunate objects of accusation.

Sir Raymond, exclaimed Brunchilda, unable longer to continue silent, What meant you by my favourite?

Let the dark conferences of the evening explain my meaning: but more than that, this business shall not thus have an end.—To you then, Duke Albert, I appeal; and, in the names of these unfortunate beings, demand a fair and equal trial. If this be refused me, I challenge you in their name; nor shall the field be quitted until one of us is slain, or justice rendered to the unfortunate.

The Duke, whose opinion of Brunchilda was at the lowest pitch, but yet who scorned suspicion, knowing it in general the mark of a little mind, declared (so earnest was he to save their lives) that he would suffer the knight to proceed in any manner he thought most just. He then commanded his fierce lady to obey.

Then, said Sir Raymond, the English knight, I command that all the party, both accusers and accused, be taken from this presence, and each placed in separate apartments until summoned to appear. The lady of Duke Albert must alone remain.

It was done as he desired.

And now, madam, I charge you by the high Lord of Heaven, by the God of mercy, truth, and justice, and by that Redeemer who was falsely accused, and whose sacred ensign I now present to you (at the same time drawing his sword, and presenting the cross thereof to Brunchilda) to swear that nothing but the truth entire shall have utterance; and that you will truly reply to such questions as I shall put unto you. I call upon you, madam, to consider you are in their presence, and will be finally by them adjudged.

Brunchilda, with her usual pride and impetuosity, refused to swear; and arose to quit the place.

END OF THE FIRST VOLUME.

COUNT RICHARD;

OR,

THE ANIMATED SKELETON

THE haughty and unbecoming behaviour of Brunchilda
in the foregoing instance, at once roused the indignation
as well as resentment of Albert; and he commanded her
to be seated, and to comply. She complied not; and Sir
Raymond, obstructing her way, calmly requested her to
be reseated; and bowing, took her hand to lead her back.
Furiously she rushed forwards to the door, demanded,
and even struggled for retreat.—To the insolence of no
man will I be subject; not even Albert unto thine, she
cried.

The Duke commanded his attendants to stop her;
and they attempted to obey him: but the violent woman
drew a dagger from her robe! She aimed a blow at Sir
Raymond; but Grimoald the Avenger starting forward,
stayed her arm.

Do not thus expose yourself, madam, said Albert to
his furious consort, who was now held upon the ground,
panting with her rage: this conduct speaks more for the
innocence of the prisoners than all your evidence has

done against it. Judgment shall now be finally given: and to you, Sir Raymond, I give the power of sentence.

Raymond replied, It appears to me so far from their being guilty, that it is my firm opinion there was some plan laid against their lives; of which, unless your lady would condescend to answer when called on in an exculpatory manner, I cannot in my own conscience venture to acquit her.

Justice is not due to the great man only; it is also for the peasant: and we may depend upon it, at the great day when the whole world is called to judgment, no respect will then be given to greatness: Princes and rulers are here but the agents of the Divinity, and sent to administer justice without alloy.—Had a plot been laid against your life, the accused would have undergone the severest scrutiny: yet you are only one, and your life but as another's. If a plot has been laid against the safety of these poor men, we should, without considering the greatness of the person, consider only the greatness of the offence: Also reflecting, that he who injures another, though the injurer be a prince, has made himself less than the other, though the injured be a peasant.—But if greatness should make any difference in our judgment, it ought only to add to its severity; for the better the education has been, so much better should be the educated; and in consequence, the greater knowledge he had of the criminality of the action, the greater wickedness must have actuated him to become guilty of it.—I do then give, as my opinion, that the Lady Brunchilda and the accusers of the men, are guilty of a secret and diabolical machination, to destroy these men, who are innocent; nor until each answers faithfully, and by their answers clear themselves from all appearance of guilt, can I forego this judgment.

The Duke looked surprized; but he consented:—the lady raved; Albert ordered her to be silent, or she should be directly bound with chains.

Never before had he shown, or had occasion for equal resolution: she therefore gave him no credit for the assertion, until the chains which had been brought to bind young Edgar were put around her, and her mouth was stopped.—Chained to a pillar, she became an object of wonder and contempt to the assembly.

The anger of Albert when once rouzed, was not easily quelled. Tho' an enemy to suspicion, he had now learned to suspect; and he made a vow, that was Brunchilda found to have been guilty, he would act by her and her companions as he should have done by Edgar, had he been the same.

Edward was then summoned; and Sir Raymond asked him at what hour he rescued the men. At three. Did the accused carry any weapons for murder? and if yes, what were they? A dagger. What dress had Dunisleda on? Green. Where did he go on his return from the convent the last night? To the lady of Duke Albert. How long did he remain with her? A few minutes only. Did he see her any more that night? No. Where did he then go? He attended on the Duke. Where went he when the Duke retired? To his chamber. Remained he there all night? Yes. At what hour did he go to his chamber? At ten. Did he see any one afterwards? He did not.

Let him be taken away, said Raymond, and produce the other.—Another being brought, Raymond demanded what weapons had the accused? Daggers. In what was Dunisleda dressed? Green. At what time were they rescued by Edward? At five. Did he see Edward yesterday? Yes. When? In the evening he also came and sat with him the over-night, after the family was retired. For what purpose? Said he was not sleepy, and did not like going to rest so early.

Take him away and bring the other, said Raymond. With the evidence of the former or Edward, the man brought forward in no point agreed, except that Dunisleda was in green. The last dress of Dunisleda was ordered to be brought; but it was not green. The wife of Grodern was then asked in what colour Dunisleda came first to her cottage? In green: but, it being wet, torn, and dirty, I persuaded her to accept that which lies before you,—was the reply she made.

It appears to me, said Grimoald, easy to account for the concordant answers of the men in respect to Dunisleda's dress.—Edward had seen her habited in it, and had certainly given the men notice, or themselves might have observed the same.

It is enough, said Albert; and we have only now to pass sentence on them.

Just then Grodern entered the church; and was asked wherefore he had fled—"To screen my grey hairs from wanton insult, did I retire: I now deliver myself, and wait thy mercy. Yet, Albert, I warn thee, consider well what thou art about; if life is taken away from any here unjustly, it will be required of thee again at the hands of thy Maker," said he.—My pleasure then, is this, replied Albert: That you, Grodern, do immediately pass sentence on Brunchilda and her accomplices, whom we hold guilty of having attempted by most wicked and malevolent practices, to take away the lives of several innocent persons. Much power I give into your hands. To do justice to the poor man, I deliver up the wife of my bosom, the princess of these domains; be just: but oh, be merciful!

Albert now hid his face in his hands, and was a while lost in sorrow: He hated vice, and mourned at the view wherever he beheld it.

Grodern, after a pause, replied, Let her pass one moon in the mysterious apartments of thy castle, and let not one of her friends be admitted to her presence; let all the rest be confined in the dungeon of the castle, and kept to hard labour for one whole year: let all the profits of their work be given to Jacquemar; and as the treacherous Edward, under the name of Alwin, was chiefly the cause of Dunisleda's death, let his property be sold, and the money given to her babes.

Albert, raising his head, said, Old man, you are merciful indeed! I feared you would have doomed her to die, and would have demanded her property. Wherefore do you ask no recompense for your own injuries?

I want not property; my son can labour; but the babes of Dunisleda have lost their mother and support: the father cannot attend to them whilst he pursues his work.—Thou askest wherefore I doomed her not to death? We have no right to deprive her of that which we did not give: life is the gift of Heaven, and Heaven alone has right to claim it back; besides, although she wished our deaths, she has not gained her wishes.

Reader, thou shalt not be delayed from other concerns, by a description of the various feelings which agitated the bosoms or coloured the features of the different people assembled in the nave when Albert confirmed this sentence; we leave thee to fancy all that malice, rage, vexation, shame, wonder, joy, and gratitude can cause, and thou wilt know all I can tell thee; for all that they could was now caused by them.

SONG

When pensive pass the lonely hours,
My harp, I seek thy pleasing pow'rs;
      Thy sprightly notes my spirits cheer.
Or tender sounds convey a charm,
Which sad afflictions oft disarm,
      And render sorrow less severe.

No female friend my hapless youth
Ere guided in the paths of truth.
      Depriv'd the gentle mother's smile,
My luckless feet might wend astray,
And wander in destruction's way:
      Vice might my innocence beguile.
But when I feel the storms arise,
And clouds obscure my temper's skies,
      I fly to thee and seek thy aid.
Emotions cease.—wild passions rest,
Tranquillity beams o'er my breast:
      Sweet harp, by thee my care's allay'd!

Thus sung Hildegarde as she struck the chords of her harp in the hall of the castle. The tears had stolen down her cheeks at the commencement of her song; reflection on her unhappy situation frequently drew them from her; but by the time she had concluded the stanzas which were dictated to her by the moment's fancy, cheerfulness had reassumed its empire, and her lovely countenance was again illumined with the smile of innocence and peace.

The present object of our attention; the Lady Hildegarde, was the only offspring of Albert and Brunchilda. In the earliest years of infancy she was deserted by her female parent, and given up entirely to the care of her attendants. Brunchilda knew not a mother's feelings; hers were of a base kind. Albert loved his little daughter; but a father's care alone cannot curb and direct sufficiently the first propensities of the infant mind. The softness and pliability of her nature would have made her imbibe easily the lessons of vice which Brunchilda would have taught her, had not she been even fortunate in her desertion. The unruly temper, imperious demeanor, impetuous passions, and unfeminine behaviour of Brunchilda, were far better hidden from her eyes than left for her to copy. Cast on the care of nurses, she was kept in distant and obscure chambers of the castle. She never saw her mother, except at those times when Albert would require the presence of his little daughter; and he would often send for her, but it was not for the purposes of instruction; it was only for his own amusement!

Albert was a good man, and detested every vice, in every form; he loved justice, and was good-tempered, but weak and superficial. This prince, therefore, could not be of much service in the education of his daughter;

which was in time trusted to an old minstrel who lived within the castle, and a grey-headed monk, who offici- ated as her confessor. She was greatly in favour with all around her: so sweet was her disposition and so contrary to Brunchilda's. Often, when marking the quick pro- gress she made in the trifles he could teach her, the old minstrel would sigh, to think so fair a blossom should remain in such a want of culture. How might the lovely Hildegarde have shone beneath a parent's care! Her person was not less charming than her mind was good. Interest and attraction seemed to hold their court round Hildegarde; and she needed but to have been generally known to have been generally loved: but happy fate! her infant years were doomed to be passed in a state of total obscurity: thus was she kept unsullied by the con- tagious breath of vice; and thus was her bosom the retreat of artless sentiment. When advance of time brought her to those years when confession was first enjoined, how delighted was the heart of her spiritual pastor, to hear her beautiful lips breathe forth nothing but the simple accents of unspotted purity! In every human breast the wayward passion will sometimes arise; but we have very little occasion really to be vexed, if we will trace every cause of our rising anger from its own origin, through its progress, to its end.

The good father had taught Hildegarde to suspend the passion whilst she reasoned on the cause:—thus ere time could give much strength to feeling, she had ob- tained placidity, and bore every cross with patience and composure. But the old monk could not live forever; and Hildegarde lost a father in her friend! His place was supplied by a stranger; and the only confidence she could place in him, was of a religious nature. The loss of the monk increased her affection for her nurse and minstrel. She would follow Fredegaire to the obscure recesses of the forest, trace the wild walks, and climb the airy summit of each surrounding hill: she would help him to bear his harp to where the waters dashed against the shore, and then, sitting by his side, listen to its sweet music: or she would bid him lead her to the rustic hamlet; she would call for the inhabitants of the cottage, and, listening to their sorrow, seek to relieve them. Often did she visit the dwelling of Jacquemar, to see her favourite Dunisleda;—and to the shelter of the ancient Grodern she would often speed: but ah! what was the charm which here could have attraction! Here she beheld the young Edgar—and here she first began to love!

But you must not love a peasant's son, would the old minstrel say.—Catching up his harp, she would reply,

> Ah me! so well I love to trace
> The beauties of my Edgar's face,
> Poor Hildegarde's heart is won,
> Although he's but a peasant's son.
>
> I seem an orphan curs'd by fate,
> Depriv'd my right to rank or state!
> My parents from their child remove!
> Then may I not a peasant love?
>
> Wilt thou, my friendly minstrel, say,
> Must I through life neglected stray,
> By all forgotten, lov'd by none,
> Unless it is the peasant's son?

When shadows long o'erstretch yon vale,
And scorching heats no more prevail.
I walk beside the torrent clear,
My peasant's rustic lays to hear.

Then, ancient minstrel, cease to chide:
My steps to Grodern's cottage guide;
For ah! my heart can love but one,
Although he is a peasant's son.

"Albert will never suffer you to marry Edgar."
'Marry him! oh heavens! I never wished for that; I only
love him best of any!'—Thus would they talk, and thus
would they ramble. The young Edgar loved in return;
his sense was strong, his understanding cultivated, his
heart was noble, and his person lovely: but he was a
peasant's son, and should not have dared to love, says
Folly!

Increase of years increased the beauty of Hildegarde;
and now the stronger and before unknown feelings
would awake: her old friend was not alive to turn them
to their proper use. Time soon removed her two other
companions. On their death she was suffered to range
over all the castle, mix in the parties, and be seen.

Brunchilda marked her opening beauty with disgust;
she feared a rival; she was the exact opposite to her
mother in every respect, even in her beauty. Brunchilda
beamed brighter than any female of the Gallic king-
doms; but would remind the gazer of some glaring
flower, which was admired for its richness and its grandeur. She wanted the superlative charm of feminine
attraction; for she wanted modesty! She might inspire

passion, but she silenced love! Hildegarde was less regu-
larly beautiful than her mother; but infinitely more
interesting. Youth and diffidence formed a sweet contrast at seventeen, to the daring countenance of
Brunchilda at thirty-nine. Where sense and good-
nature lighted up the countenance of the one, it was
vivacity and passion which glowed in the visage of the
other:—one had the soft lustre of the evening-star, the
other the fierce blaze of the meridian sun. Benevolence
smiled in the mild eyes of Hildegarde; but in the fero-
cious look of the mother, vanity and the love of
conquest raged.

Albert now began to view his daughter no longer as
a plaything; he saw the hatred of Brunchilda, and
wished to recompense it by his superior attention: and
now he undertook to instruct her himself in what he
could. Amply did her mind repay his care; and the
flowers of improvement luxuriantly bloomed upon the
lovely scion. From the gay hall and giddy circle, often
would Brunchilda bid her be absent: she dreaded such a
rival there. This was no punishment to Hildegarde,
who, though she had that natural love of sociality which
is attendant on youth, health, and sprightliness, had it so
tempered with diffidence and discretion, that she of-
tener tried to shun than seek those scenes of dissipation.
Poor Hildegarde wanted some female friend: she had
attendants appointed her, and a suit of apartments dedi-
cated to her use; but she was not satisfied. In that court
of vice few females could remain unsullied; and the ladies appointed to wait on Hildegarde, found her
company what they termed too insipid, to pay her much
attention. These therefore could not become the confi-

dants of the young lady, whose unguarded situation grew now doubly painful; for she became the object of illicit love.

Count Richard scorned all ties which gave disappointment to his wishes: he shunned all whom he might attain, to indulge the depravity of his temper; which led him only to wish for such as were forbidden by honour, justice, and morality. Possibly, had Hildegarde been nowise related to him, nor by her union with any other, prevented from receiving his addresses, he would have looked on her without passion, and passed by regardless, anxious to engage in some more vile pursuit; but now, as morality forbade him to love Hildegarde, she was the only lady he was most strongly determined resolutely to love. To Brunchilda did the Count declare his wishes; and by her they were approved. Envious of a virtue which she had not the resolution to copy, she was desirous of seeing her daughter sunk as deep in infamy as herself.

The Count was too wily to suffer the Duke to discover his disposition: Albert was not overstocked with penetration, and he seldom suspected what he did not immediately see. Hildegarde knew not the temper of her uncle: she scarcely understood his declarations; for him to offer her love, was a circumstance she so little thought possible, that when he actually did so, she fancied the fumes of liquor had disturbed his brain, or that she had not entirely comprehended his real meaning. If she ever refused patiently to listen to him, or gave him the slightest repulse, she immediately drew on herself the sharp anger of Brunchilda. Hildegarde could not mention it to her father, for she knew not what to declare, though she frequently mentioned her dislike of him. Her only resource was, in spending as much time in her own apartments as was possible. On the day of the trial, having asked of one of her female attendants, who those were that had gone to the convent, the lady (who was in the pay and interest of Count Richard, and had been ordered by him to say he was absent) informed her every person was from home, saving a few old domestics and a portion of the guards. A short time before the party came back from the trial, Hildegarde, thinking herself free from unpleasant company, ordered her harp into her favourite hall. Sometimes the melancholy situation she was in, the treatment of her mother, and perplexing conduct of her uncle, drew tears from her eyes:—such was now the case, and this it was which prompted her to sing.

Although Fridegaire had taught her music, he never could teach her poetry; and it is not for the beauty of her composition that the lines are inserted, but merely to show the feelings of her mind.

Scarcely had she finished when Count Richard entered the hall. She started at his presence, and appeared displeased. She would have quitted the place that minute, but she feared to affront him, for she knew he was malicious; but she intended to do so the moment she could, without its appearing that, in quitting the hall, she sought to leave his presence.—He looked on her with a daring gaze, with fierce and impatient eyes, which he tried to soften with the tenderness of love; but still there lurked behind his smile a ferocity which terrified the gentle Hildegarde.—Count Richard might grin, but he could not look tender.—A man who had never known one virtuous or endearing emotion, who had ever been a stranger to real love, pity or affection, could ill attempt to make his countenance express what his heart could never feel.

The Count observed the terror his presence and countenance occasioned; and this strengthened his resolution, for his malignant heart loved even to terrify the objects whom he thought were in his power. Still in the present instance he wished this timid girl not to be warned of his purposes by his looks, for she was entirely at his mercy: her manifest dislike stimulated him to injure her, from the spirit of revenge. Never yet could he find one female that could truly love him; many fearing his power, or, from sordid motives, had become his prey; but none from love. This made him swear in his own heart enmity to the whole female sex; and he was determined to add every aggravation to that enmity which his fancy could suggest.

To dissipate the present terror of Hildegarde, that she might the more easily fall into the snare he was spreading for her, he took her harp, and playing, began to sing to it. This was a charm she scarcely could resist, for Richard had an excellent voice, and he could draw tones from the instrument which would make attention start. He sung of wars and bloody deeds, of fairies and enchanted legends. Well pleased that he confined himself to music, Hildegarde listened, and forgot her fear, until suddenly putting aside the harp, he threw himself on his knees before her, and, seizing both her hands, asked, whilst she struggled to release them, wherefore she ever wished to shun his presence, and showed so much dislike whenever he approached.

'Because you talk so strange to me, and look so fierce.'

"I only tell you, Hildegarde, how much I love you; and why should you shun any thing which loves you?"

'But you are my uncle,' said she again, trying to extricate her hands.

"Ah, Hildegarde! how often have I heard you say you wished Brunchilda would love you! and why do not you wish that I should also?"

'I need not wish it, when you say you do.'

"Then, why hate me for it? You love your little dog, Fidelle, and your faithful lamb, who loves you too. Oh, Hildegarde! if you would but love and caress me half as much as either of them!"

'They deserve to be loved, because they only try to amuse and please me:—you teize me.'

"Tell me what I shall do to make you love me?"

'Let me go away now.'

"No, that I cannot do; my sister bade me take care of you this morning."

'Let me go to my chamber.'

"I will if you will caress me first, as you do Fidelle, and let me follow you there, as he follows you."—Thus saying, he attempted to embrace her; but breaking from him, she was running toward her apartments, when the horn sounded at the castle-gates, which foretold the return of Albert. Richard disappointed, departed from the hall, and Hildegarde, not wishing to see her mother, retired uneasy, terrified, and uncertain what to do.

And now the Duke and his train entered the castle. Brunchilda was loosed from her palfrey, on which, with chains, she had been bound. For a few nights Albert proposed deferring the confinement of Brunchilda to the haunted chambers: he agreed to suffer her to remain well guarded in her own apartments until something had been done to the others to make them habitable. He ordered some workmen to open them on the morrow, and prepare them for the reception of Brunchilda: he determined that night, notwithstanding the adventure of the last, to again encounter the ghosts. The two knights made no objection to his proposal, but rather waited with impatience to discover the causes of their former surprize.

It soon became known to Count Richard, of the fate of his sister, part of whose infamous transactions were for his sake. To the anger he already nursed against Albert, he now added that which was raised by the above affair; and more deeply was he resolved upon the murder of his host: and this, not from the love he had for Brunchilda (and who could love such a sister) but from the hatred he bore to the Duke. It became doubly necessary for him to conceal his determination, as he might well suppose, that to have betrayed by voice, countenance, or manner the least trace of it, he should be confined with his sister, or banished the court. He was not suffered to see Brunchilda on his return, neither could he obtain an interview with any of her chief favourites or train: all were secured for the present. Half devoured with malice and the effects of concealed rage, he hid himself in his apartment, where he spent most of the remainder of the day preparing the plan for the execution of his revenge. From the lessons of his mother Gunilda, he had learnt to compose the most subtle poisons; to determine the degree of their effect and torture, and even the hour of their operation. He now busied himself in preparing one which should be accompanied in its effect (which was fixed for a few hours after it had been taken) with the most poignant agonies; neither could any remedy be found sufficiently speedy or strong to counteract its baneful effects. The disgust which had been raised in the bosom of Duke Albert by the late shameless conduct of Brunchilda, had long made him cease to sleep in her apartments: those he now used were at a distance from any others, which were filled on the night after his return from the trial. The rooms which adjoined his had been slept in on the preceding night; but, immediately that Brunchilda was condemned, every person who had been a visitor at the castle, thought they could not with propriety continue longer; and by their presence add to the pain the merciful Albert must naturally feel on the punishment of one who was still his wife, although she was never dear to him. The knights offered to quit the castle also; but this was not permitted by Albert, who earnestly requested their presence for some time longer. He had now risen high in the opinion of the English Raymond; and even Grimoald the Avenger began to fancy that the Duke was almost honest.

The distance that Albert slept from any person, now made Count Richard think he could more easily atchieve his infamous intention; yet he feared that alone he could not overpower the Duke, unless assisted: he therefore made known his purpose to a servant who had ever been ready to assist him in any nefarious undertaking. Gondemar (which was the name of this minion) was therefore sworn to a strict secrecy; and under the promise of a great reward, undertook to assist him. Richard attended not at supper; he pleaded sorrow for the ill conduct of his sister, and remained above.

Albert being left at table alone with Grimoald and Raymond, thought it proper to question the latter on an expression which he had let fall during the examination of the morning. The word *favourite* had rested on his ear, and made a deep impression. He remarked Brunchilda's anger on the application of it, with the little notice she seemed to wish to take of the reply.— Had a woman been conscious of virtue, she would have demanded an explanation:—had Raymond refused, she might justly have regarded him as a coward and a villain: for can a man be less, who before or to others would darkly attack the character of a female, and when called on to explain, refuse to do her justice? Brunchilda had found Raymond more ready to reply; and that in such a manner, as she found it her interest to prevent. She had therefore gladly preserved a temporary silence, and suffered him to proceed. This, as before was remarked, escaped not the notice of Albert; who was anxious to know what could be meant by the expression. He therefore demanded of Raymond the meaning of his speech, and his reasons for making it: what also were the "dark conferences" he alluded to.—Raymond readily replied; for he was too generous ever to make an accusation of any person of whose guilt he was not beforehand fully convinced.

Last night, whilst I waited for your approach (said Raymond) I heard some footsteps passing the gallery, at a distance from my chamber: imagining it to be yourself, and eager to attend you, I gently opened the door of my room; but I beheld Edward, who, without seeing me, entered the apartments of your lady, accompanied by the two men we have been trying, and who appeared against the innocent men we have acquitted. Not long after, I heard them retire. I again gently opened my door: I saw them departing, but Edward remained. Surely, Albert, these private meetings could have been for no purposes but those of evil; and surely I was justified in using the expressions which I did.

Base, perfidious woman! exclaimed Albert; the mysterious appearances or noises of the haunted chambers, are probably occasioned by her wickedness, and by her contrivance: but those rooms shall not be her prison for a month alone, but throughout her life: her own goblins shall be her own and sole source of amusement. Never could I bring my heart yet to love her. Honour and tenderness for a woman, and a wife's feelings, led me to conceal this from her. I tried to treat her, as if I loved. I have indulged her in every wish, and prevented every want. By a parent who preferred my enrichment to my happiness was I forced to marry her: when I espoused her I loved another, beautiful and amiable, as Brunchilda is the reverse: she is now lost to me for ever: beneath the veil of a nun she now, in a distant clime, mourns a love which was mutual and unhappy. On my marriage with Brunchilda I became possessed of all these extensive domains; but of this castle I have never until now been master: I have most unfortunately, ever since I wedded Brunchilda, through a mistaken attachment which I conceived on her part, suffered her to rule both me and mine with an absolute sway.—But let us waste no more time on so unworthy a subject; let us cease to talk of her, and proceed to the chambers: let us take this time each a separate light, lest the ghost should again leave us in the dark, by blowing out the Avenger's.

It may appear strange or unreasonable, that the Duke should prefer the night to the day for the discovery of the disturbers of his castle's quiet; but as he began to imagine the report of ghosts was entirely occasioned by the nocturnal revels of Brunchilda, or some designing people, he supposed the time of night was most likely to surprise them in. Had he gone in the day, it would have given them a warning of what he intended, at a time when it was best they should be left in a seemingly total security.

According to Albert's proposal, though rather to the mortification of Grimoald, they each carried a separate light. The Avenger felt his pride much hurt at the supposition or rather recollection of his dropping that he carried on the preceding night, from alarm. They met this time with neither interruption, alteration, nor ghost, through any of the apartments of the north wing, until they came to the skeleton's bed-chamber:—they found the door closed. The Duke was first and opened it: on doing which, a small piece of paper fell at his feet. Picking it up and unfolding it, he found written therein, "Guard thine own life, guard Hildegarde. To what end deprivest thou the lioness of her power, if thou sufferest the lion to roam at liberty?"

For some time they pondered over the lines: they appeared inexplicable; but they were better saved than lost, and the Duke secured them. He then turned his attention to the chamber. The bed and every thing else appeared as on the preceding night, but no signs of a skeleton; they examined the room thoroughly, and on the floor discovered the traces of blood, which must have been spilt many years before, and which ran in such quantities as to cover a large space. In one spot near the door it had congealed and formed a rising on the floor. At a distance from the bed, and on the ground, lay a large silver cup; which appeared to have been thrown down with some violence, from a bruise on the side, and which had not been removed for a long time. It was with some difficulty they discovered it was silver, as dust and tarnish obscured all its brightness. The floor was stained near where it had fallen, with a dark coloured liquor; but they could not discover of what nature it was, the mark itself being scarcely discernible, from time and dirt. Various conjectures were formed on these appearances: they remarked, some foul murder must have been committed; and suspicion alighted on the former relatives of Brunchilda who inhabited the castle: but to find out who was the injured person, and who the injurer, they deemed impossible. From the dark bosoms of the Count or his sister, they fancied they could never draw it; and would never have the power to do justice to those persons who might still remain related to or interested in the concerns of the deceased. Grimoald, with much petulance and assumed consequence, declared he should make it his business to enquire; and would himself question Brunchilda. Indeed, he asserted, he deemed it his duty to insist on the Duke's permission to interrogate that lady and her brother; and he had no doubt he should do it so skilfully, that they could not evade the truth, especially as he never met with a ghost yet which he did not discover the meaning of, or drive away.

Most likely, said Raymond, if (as I have before heard you assert) they were commonly only rats and owls. But which do you reckon conqueror last night,—the rat which made you drop the lamp, the owls which sung while you fought in the bog, or yourself?

Grimoald angrily replied, there was no time for trifling; but he would at some future period convince the incredulous Englishman of his consequence and valour. You know not, said he, but what I myself may be the person injured by these murders.

And pray, who are you? asked Albert.

Grimoald the Avenger! replied Raymond, laughing.

I am, Sir knight, and I will prove it, retorted the angry incognito, stalking most pompously out of the room.

Nothing more occurred this night in the haunted chambers; and they retired uninterrupted from the north wing, after waiting in vain for the appearance of some apparition.

Having spent great part of the night in the wing, and being more inclined to talk than sleep, they retired silently to the apartments of the Duke, fearing their voices should be overheard.

No sooner were they entered, than from behind some pieces of furniture rushed Count Richard, bearing a poniard and a cup. He started back on seeing the two knights, as from their quiet entry he thought none but the Duke had come in. He soon recovered himself; and throwing from him the cup, from which in the action of starting he spilt some liquor, he sprang forward, and with the poniard aimed a blow at Albert; but he struck him not; the knights seized him before he could effect his purpose; but struggling violently, he disengaged one arm, with which he drew another poniard from his bosom, and plunged it in the side of Sir Raymond, who with the other knight, had gone this evening unarmed. The reason they had armed themselves the night before was, that they apprehended some treachery from the Duke; but now no longer suspecting him, and having only merry ghosts to encounter, they fancied there was little occasion for much caution.

By the assistance of Albert the Count was again secured; but his uncommon strength rendered it a difficulty to perform. Raymond in a few minutes complained he was no longer able to assist them; his side felt unusually painful; the poniard he knew had not struck far; but he never had a wound of equal agony, or which caused such a heat in the place, or faintness in his body. Their distress on losing his help was very great; it was impossible they could quit Richard to assist him; and without him they could not manage the furious assassin. They could have killed him; but this the Duke would not admit of: he wanted to preserve his life for a confession which he now was certain would bring some atrocities to light. They tried to drag him to the other parts of the castle, where they could call for help; but in vain, his struggles prevented them.

Stab him, said Grimoald.

Surely not, replied Albert; let him live, repent, and confess.

"In the haunted apartments," said a voice behind them, at the sound of which Richard trembled and turned quite pale, "Assistance is now at hand." Again, said the voice, (Richard lost his strength, and sunk on the ground, trembling and aghast) "Count Richard shall revenge Count Richard's wrongs."

At these words of the voice the terrified Count gave one desperate struggle, and, breaking from them, rushed towards the door, his hair nearly upright, and his looks wild and ghastly:

In the general surprize occasioned by hearing of the voice, and Richard's uncommon terror, those who held him had in part relinquished their hold, which enabled him to shake them from him and escape thus far: but though he had broken from them, it was of little avail, because at the door he was arrested by two of the Duke's domestics, whom the most fortunate but unusual chance had directed thither on some business of small consequence.

"Stop him," said the voice, again close to him: and the servants seeing his furious demeanor, obeyed their invisible director.

They now altogether conveyed him to his chamber; where they chained him down.

"This must be the Lion," said Grimoald, "which the paper bid you beware of: but where is Sir Raymond?"

They immediately returned to seek for him, and discovered that he had not passed to many chambers distant from the Duke's, when he was obliged to rest: excess of pain and uncommon illness prevented his continuing; he was unable to stand, and seemed almost dying.

They examined his wound, and found it inflamed in some places, and black in others.

"I could almost fancy I felt the certain approaches of death," said the fainting Raymond; "that villain's dagger was most surely poisoned."

They administered every remedy they could; and relief began to spread its cheering influence over the worthy knight.

Some hasty rumourers informed Hubert that Sir Raymond was dead. On hearing of it he smiled a smile peculiar to himself, full fraught with the triumph of malignancy. That poisoned dagger was intended for Duke Albert, said he, in case I could not force him to drink of the cup which I had prepared for him.

Infernal villain! exclaimed Grimoald, who had heard his speech; I would this minute kill thee, and banish thy vile soul from the earth which thou encumberest, wert thou not reserved for greater torments.

I scorn thy threats, vain boaster, replied the Count: I will not exist one moment beyond my own pleasure: thou mayest kill, but thou canst not keep me alive, when fate, dependent on my own will, has fixed the moment of my death.

The morning had now dawned long upon them, and they were debating how they should act, when one of the attendants of the Lady Hildegarde rushed in, crying out, and apparently almost frantic, Oh! where is my lady? give me the Lady Hildegarde!

What is the matter? asked the Duke.—Oh, my lady is gone! my lady is gone! oh, I have looked everywhere, but know not whither she is gone!

Count Richard smiled his favourite smile; the Duke demanded an explanation, bidding her be quiet, and cease those violent actions and exclamations which she used. At this she only screamed and howled the more, until Albert began to suspect there was some design in her immoderate and unnatural outcries. He could gain no intelligence from her, but that Hildegarde was gone. On finding this the case, he ordered one of his attendants and Grimoald to stay with her and the Count whilst he went himself to discover what could be the meaning of her behaviour. He found Hildegarde actually missing; neither could he in any part of the castle discover her. He then returned to the lady and Count Richard, and again demanded her to give him a calm account of all she knew; but he found her in a state which was little likely to admit of her giving a regular detail of any thing: she was held fast by Grimoald and the attendant, panting with fury and anger. Having asked the reason, he was answered by the knight, "Soon after you departed, not thinking it of any consequence to remain here, as Count Richard was secure, and supposing I should be of use to you in finding your daughter, I left the room; but had not gone many paces when I heard the noise of a violent scuffle, and the attendant's voice calling me back. I returned, and found him struggling with the lady, to wrest from her grasp a dagger. With him I effected this, and heard from him, that immediately on my departure, she had drawn the dagger from her robe, and, holding it in one hand, advanced to the Count, and kneeling down, attempted to unloose a part of his chains which appeared most easy; and that seeing this, your attendant tried to get from her the dagger; which occasioned the noise I had heard.

Upon hearing this, Albert, without any real or settled intention of murdering the lady, took the dagger; and being highly exasperated, held it to her bosom, vowing to stab her to the heart that instant if she did not confess the meaning of her behaviour, and where Hildegarde was. The lady, terrified, and not possessing courage equal to her undertaking, soon informed him that Hildegarde was actually gone away: that she went, as usual, to wait on her lady in the morning, and found her missing; and that hearing that Richard was confined, she judged she could turn the loss of the Lady Hildegarde to some use: that she was in the pay of Richard, who had bribed her to admit him to the chamber of his niece, and that, having let him in at night, she left him with the lady:—that finding her gone in the morning, and the Count confined, and no tidings of Hildegarde, she thought that if she raised an outcry and bustle in the castle, every person would quit the Count to search for the lady; at which time, were she left with Richard, she could have an opportunity of unfastening his chains. Being left alone with only one attendant, she imagined her dagger would intimidate and prevent him from hindering her in the liberation of the Count.

"Villain," cried the Duke to Count Richard, "where, where is my daughter? your hellish agents have stolen her from me!"

Richard smiled; and the malice of a demon marked upon his visage.

Albert ordered the lady to be close confined, vowing torments should be used to make them confess, if milder usage would not do. The mild good-natured Duke now had become a man of rage and violence. It was not a little which in general could rouse his temper; but when it was done, he could equal Richard. Notwithstanding every thing he could urge or threaten, the Count determined to be silent. He then called for the attendants of Richard, to try if they were less wicked, less cruel, than their master. They all came, except one. Richard now broke silence.—Where is Gondemar? he sternly asked: but none could give any other reply than that Gondemar was missing.—Hell and madness! exclaimed he furiously, looking nearly all that Hell or madness could look: but in a minute he recovered his recollection, and smiled again. The fears of the Duke made him immediately fancy that at the commands of Richard, Gondemar had carried off his daughter; though by what means, or through what avenue she could escape, was improbable for him to guess: it was impossible to escape from the walls or windows of the castle; and by the gates she had not been. Rage and grief swayed by turns the soul of the unhappy father. Sometimes he was silent, sometimes he raved; but long was he incapable of judging how he should proceed, or what was fittest to be done. At length, by the advice of Grimoald, he determined to confine Count Richard immediately to the haunted rooms, and waste no more time in preparing them for the reception of Brunchilda. Richard was accordingly conveyed thither, and carefully chained, but in an apartment far separate from that of his sister.

The malice and vexation which agitated the bosom of the Count was now of no avail to him, and he was obliged, unheeded and detested, to fume out the remainder of his fury totally alone in a large, old, dusty, and decayed chamber: the worst and most solitary which could be found in that wing had been allotted him. Nothing was allowed him but some mouldy rushes for a bed, and a scanty quantity of coarse provision for his sustenance. A small allowance of wood was placed near him, and an iron pan, in which his fire was made. Through pride and vexation, his fire he for some time neglected; but at length the rain and wind, which came through the cracks in the decayed walls, made him turn his attention to the pan—in which the embers were almost expired.

Finding, after some time, that anger would neither loosen his chains nor give him the rest he had lost in planning and attempting to perform diabolical schemes for the two last nights, he became willing to seek it on his rushes. The dark hours of night began to gloom around him; and he was allowed no light but what might arise from the glare of his fire. His wood was all expended except a few small sticks; these he carefully placed on the pan, almost doubting which was the worst, the excessive chillness of the evening, or the smoke which annoyed him; and which (there being no chimney in the room) only made its exit through some of the crevices in the walls made by the rage of time. The grafted windows at the top of the room, had been boarded up; and very little light or air could pass through them, unless in consequence of partial decay. There were some eyelet holes in the walls; but these, for some reason, had been stopped up. The whole place bore the appearance of a dungeon, so contrived that neither sound nor sight could enter.

Overcome with fatigue, heightened by the vain ef-forts of his fury, Richard laid himself down and essayed to sleep; a few broken slumbers would occasionally steal over him, but guilt drove full far away the sweets of sound sleep. From one of his slumbers he was awakened by a noise in his room; when turning his head to from whence it proceeded, he beheld the iron pan drawn to a distance from him, and a skeleton sitting by it. The appearance had a double portion of horror, because the light which was caused by the embers was too feeble to strike to advantage upon any but near objects: the chamber, in consequence, seemed almost entirely dark, except in the spot on which sat the skeleton. The Count, in amazement and horror, started up, and attempted to rush forwards, to dash in pieces the phantom which awaked him, but a sudden pull backwards robbed him of the power; at the same time the skeleton moved further from him, and as it went backwards drew along with it, by grasping it with its long and uncased fingers, the iron-pan. Sinking again upon his rushes in an agony of terror, he hid his face in his hands, unable to bear the strangeness of the spectacle; but he found, on their noise having restored him partly from his fright, that it was nothing but his chains which had caused the sudden pull: they were fastened to an iron in the wall, and by their not giving way, caused the resistance. For a while he continued hiding his face with his hands; but a noise like raking the ashes in the pan, made him again start up; but he only did so again to sink, overwhelmed with horror at a sight far more surprising and perplexing than what he had last beheld.

The figure of the real Count Richard stood before him: the man on whose reported banishment he had assumed the title and property he now possessed under his name.

In one hand the figure held a dagger, with which he was stirring up the embers, as if to cause a brighter light to illuminate the chamber. In his other hand he held a cup. In a voice harsh and vindictive, and which made every nerve in the system of the trembler reverberate, the figure addressed him with, "Knowest thou this cup, proud Hubert?"

Again with his shaking hands Hubert hid his face.— "Regard me," said the form, "or this hour, this minute shall be thy last."

Hubert just dared to raise his head.

"Usurper," continued it, "wilt thou chuse for thy portion this dagger in thy bosom, or wilt thou suck in thy death from this cup, by which thou didst attempt to perpetrate my death? Yes, villain, this is the very cup which, when attended by the infamous Gunilda, thou gavest to my grasp."

Hubert became unable to answer; and the form continued:—I leave thee this night for thy repentance: to-morrow night shall give thee to eternity.—It said nothing more, but immediately, taking the skeleton by one hand, he dashed over the pan of fire, and darkness took place of partial gloom:—no more noise was heard; but the pangs of guilt weighed too heavy on the soul of Hubert to permit it to rise above the terrors of the scene and the accusations of a burdened conscience:—he sunk beneath them; fear locked up all his senses, and produced a swoon.

Of what has often been mistaken for and by the world falsely termed courage, Hubert possessed an ample share; for if ferociously slaughtering our enemies, dashing forwards in the heat of battle, or in the knightly joust, be courage, then all these would Hubert do. Where high towering ambition, hasty rage, hot enthusiasm, or deep revenge instigates the soul to daring actions; when our enemies are to be overthrown, or popular applause is to reward our actions, we can ill deem it courage. No, it is ambition, rage, enthusiasm, or revenge: but to cool courage Hubert was a stranger; for conscience could make him tremble like an infant at the powerless form; and such he thought the figure of Count Richard.

The improbability of a spirit's having power to act upon this earth, or to grasp and carry heavy and material substances, never passed his mind: to see the figure of a man he had himself, as he thought, given certain death to, now stand before him, bearing the very implements of revenge which himself had borne, and hearing him pronounce his doom, was that occupied the mind of Hubert, and left him in a doubt and terror of he knew not what.

Long he lay in the swoon. When he recovered he found himself in total darkness: slumber no more visited his eyes, fear kept him awake, and he lay trembling until the morning-light showed him the pan standing exactly where it had done at the spectre's exit, but overturned; and no appearance of any thing else whatever: no change had taken place in the door or walls; and there was no appearance of the least opening by which any thing but a ghost could enter.

He now began to revive from his terror. Sometimes he wished to and almost did think it had been all nothing but a horrible dream: but again the removal and overthrow of the iron-pan perplexed him greatly. Sometimes he would think it the effect of goblins; and at others, that he had by some means done it himself, in an action of rage during his sleep: yet this could not have been, unless he had taken it up and dashed it to that distance.

At ten in the morning Grimoald entered the chamber of confinement, and brought with him some cakes of coarse flour. He was soon after followed by one of the Duke's servants, who brought him water, and a supply of wood; and who placed the pan in its former situation, and lighted his fire. They enquired by what means the pan had come in the situation they found it; but no answer was returned to their question; the consequence of which was, that new chains were fastened on him, as they feared himself had done it, and, by some flaw in the old chains, he had been enabled to move from the corner where his bed was placed, and would at other times have it in his power to escape.

In every instance, it was doomed for Richard to find that his impolitic obstinacy punished none so greatly as himself, as it redoubled the efforts of those he injured by it, to overcome him.

Presently the Duke entered the apartment.—The altered countenance of Hubert was remarked by him; for on it fear and the anguish of his conscience had left a deep impression. Albert imputed the alteration to the remorse which guilt almost invariably occasions, and to the apprehension he might naturally feel of the reward he merited. Taking advantage of what to him seemed a favourable circumstance, he again began to interrogate.—Where is my daughter, caitiff? demanded the Duke. Hubert smiled, looked malicious, but gave no reply.—Count Richard, dost thou still determine not to answer? and wilt thou still dare me to perform my threats of torture and of death? continued he.

Fear not, replied a voice; he will not dare to die!

Each present recognised the sound: it was the voice of wonder and gladness to three, because it had once brought them succour; but to Hubert it was only that of horror, for it was the voice of the murdered Richard. Violently did it cause him to tremble; and the perspiration of fear, in large drops stole down his visage.

What guilt is this upon thy soul, that agitates thee thus? asked Albert.

Hubert replied only with a hollow groan, whilst he ground his teeth and knit his brows with fury, horror, and dismay.

Some strange dark mystery lurks behind this scene of terror! Oh my child, my child, my Hildegarde, what can be thy fate? Torn from the protection of a parent's roof, who can, who will defend thee? exclaimed the distressed sire of the lost fair one, whilst he wrung his hands in undescribable agony.

She lives! uttered Hubert in a low voice, gloomily pronounced through his clenched teeth, at the same time casting his eyes on the Duke with a malicious sneer.

As a flash of brilliant lightning did this speech irradiate the countenance of Albert; who falling at the feet of the Count, was for a moment speechless; but at length burst from his heart, Oh tell me she is safe, uninjured, and I forgive thy every crime. Oh where, where is she?

The sneer of malice still more strongly impressing the visage of the wretch from whence it had not passed during the agitation of Albert, he replied.—

Far, far from thy power; but she is yet in mine. I promise you she is safe! and if to tear her from each vulgar peasant's arms, and reserve her but for one is not an injury, she is yet uninjured; but wherefore, cruel father, would you rend the willing beauty from my care, and from a love she has so oft solicited?

An agony of parental suffering almost suffocated the Duke, who, starting up, exclaimed, Oh powers of utterance, teach me a word to fit this fiend, this eldest born of Hell!—Wretch, villain, monster, if thou darest to harm her, the bitterest torments be thy portion. Unspotted as the holy virgin, how darest thou even pronounce her name! say instantly where thou hast conveyed her, or the keenest pangs the rack and fire can give thee shall be thine.

Like water to the thirsty palate, sweet as my favour to the amorous, the sighing Hildegarde, will thy sufferings, Albert, be to me, whilst I am on that rack: each groan thou utterest for thy daughter's honour will be the healing balm to me!

Unable to reply, Albert rushed forward to prepare the tortures; but his passage was intercepted, and Hildegarde sprang into his arms.

Here, reader, let us pause a while; let us not interrupt the parent's transport or the daughter's joy: they both are sacred! After the scene of horrors we have viewed, the mind steals gladly from the chilling prospect, and rests its weary eyes upon delight.

> Memory unheeded for a while pass by;
>   Let the soul sink in sympathetic joy.
> Sad retrospection, yet withhold the sigh,
>   Nor yet the momentary bliss destroy.
>   Too evanescent are the tranquil gleams;
> Sorrow too quickly wakes to woe the mind:
> We wake to recollection, and to find
> The gay enchanting prospects faded with our rest,
> And all but empty, idle, and at best,
>   False, flatt'ring dreams

"And art thou really safe, my daughter, or is this but an illusion of the overcharged mind, which makes me think thee here?" were the first words uttered by the Duke, who was assured by the beloved of his soul, she was really safe.

The most bitter execrations escaped from the mouth of Hubert, who seemed in agony at a sight so distant from his wishes; but he remained totally disregarded for a while by the reunited sufferers, who gave way to curiosity and joy. Enquiries, on the part of Albert and replies on that of Hildegarde, were equally interesting to all others present. Hubert was therefore left stretched on the rack of his own disappointed malice, whereby he suffered far severer tortures than any Albert could inflict.

Tell me, said the Duke, my beloved Hildegarde, by what magic, or what power divine I here behold thee!

Ah, surely, my father, from the regions of enchant-
ment am I come. Behold that villain, iniquitous Count
Richard; he has been the original cause, and some kind
ghost the secondary. The night before last, at an early
hour, whilst you were busied in the search of these mysterious apartments (for here I am informed you were)
that villain came to my chamber; and one of my female
attendants who was then with me, and whom he must
have suborned for the purpose, let him in on his gently
tapping at the door; and who quitted the room at the
same time, and closed the door after her. Long has he
urged the most infamous of suits: and little, until lately,
did I comprehend his meaning; so little did I imagine
any one could be so truly despicable. But with him the
ties of affinity are as cobwebs, or he had not dared to
insult me with his incestuous passion.—It would now be
too tedious to tell you all his conduct; suffice it to say I
have ever treated him with ridicule, and when understood, with anger.—Astonished and angry at this proof
of his insolence, I bade him instantly quit the apartment.
Without appearing abashed, he went towards the door, I
thought to leave me; but instead of obeying my command, he turned the key, and then placed it in his
bosom. He then again advanced, and intreated me to
listen; but in vain: for far from being able to attend, I
was too much terrified to scream: fear and surprise at the
monster's last action had almost chained up my senses.
Alas, my father, what did I not suffer, when I knew
well, my voice, should I call for assistance, was too weak
to be heard, as my chamber lay so remote from all.—Ah,
never let me again be placed at such a distance from the
family, and so near to danger!—Finding me silent, he

continued his detestable discourse, until recovering, in some measure, from the first shock of terror, I again bade him begone:—but he advanced still nearer, and used threatening language.—Whence now was help to come! To Heaven, in that moment of sad calamity, I cried; thence alone expecting aid.—Determined no longer to give me respite, the villain seized me; and I screamed without a second hope, but in the deep anguish of despair. At that instant a voice from behind us, called aloud, "Miscreant, retreat! look but on me!"

The Count started, and instantly quitting his prey, turned round and beheld a man in complete armour, a sword was in his hand unsheathed! The figure drew near:—My uncle sunk upon the earth, and exclaimed, 'Count Richard!'

"Rise, villain," said my delivering spirit, "and depart; but in the crime thou hast yet in thy heart, expect my interruption! Hildegarde is my care."

The trembling wretch drew from his bosom the key of my chamber, and departed. The armed apparition then raised a pannel I had never observed (and which is made of wood, but so coloured as to appear like the walls) and led me through, bidding me not to fear. His advice was useless; I was nearly fainting with apprehension, and therefore hesitated to proceed. Come forward, Hildegarde, for thou needest a protector, said my guardian ghost; I only lead thee hence to protect thee from further wrongs: I want thee to confront this wretch when time is ripe.—Then taking my arm, which I no longer refused him, he led me through many dark passages and down many steps, until I felt weary; at length he lodged me in a room which appeared like the cell of some convent. Here I remained; and a venerable old woman brought me food and slept in the same cell, both that and last night, but would never give me any other answer to my various enquiries, than "rest quiet, amiable Hildegarde, Heaven, under whose protection thou art, will discover all."

Oh no, my father, I forgot: one question she did reply to. I asked how thou wert, if safe, and where? She replied, "searching the haunted wing, and proceeding to justice!"

This was some relief to my anxiety; but my curiosity was insatiable. I once said, 'do, tell me what or who that ghost in armour was: now only answer that;' and she sat down and laughed heartily at me. This morning the same armed spirit appeared again, and, leading me through several passages, declared he was going to deliver me to you; but first made me, by dint of gentle intreaty, suffer my eyes to be bound round; which I did, as I had been hitherto so well and kindly treated by him. I soon found myself in a room not far removed from this; where he left me, bidding me wait until he gave me orders to unbind my eyes; which he promised shortly to do; and in about a quarter of an hour he returned to me and unbound them himself: he then pointed to a door which was open, and ordered me to proceed that way through the apartments which were open, until I heard your voice, which should be my direction to you.—"And fear not although you hear the voice of Count Richard," added he; "for he is harmless now!"—And thus, my dear sire, am I once more restored to your paternal arms.

In speechless ecstasy the happy Albert again embraced his daughter. Rapture being somewhat subsided, he said, 'Good Heavens! my dear Hildegarde, and to think that yonder villain, to torture my soul, declared thou wast yet in his power!"

"Mind him not:" said Grimoald, who had hitherto been a silent spectator of the scene; "he is now in ours." 'He is now in mine,' said the real Count Richard, entering at the same moment, and advancing towards Hubert.

"Ah Heavens! my guardian ghost, my guardian ghost!" exclaimed Hildegarde, seizing his steel-clad hand, and kissing the cold gauntlet.

Hubert was not so much elated at his sight: he groaned and cast himself upon the earth, hiding his face with his hands, and beneath his cloke; which he cast over his head.

'He is now in mine,' said the son of Grodern, who also appeared beside him; but not clad as usual in his homely weeds, but dressed as became the offspring of nobility. His noble person and beautiful, but then commanding visage, drew their regards; Surprise's self became weary with repeated calls; and they ceased to wonder where all appeared so strange. But although they beheld him, his change of dress prevented their discovering or guessing, who he was.

'I will revenge my parents wrongs——.'

He was proceeding, when the shrill voice of an enraged female called their attention from the present scene, and speedily rushed into the room, Brunchilda nearly raving.

"Yes I, I, I will release him," she exclaimed, sinking down exhausted with rage, on the rushes near Count Richard. Her guards soon followed, and were attempting to seize her, when, starting up again, she drew a dagger from her robe, and rushed upon the Duke, trying to bury it in his heart; but partly aware of her design, he had so far leant backwards as to prevent the full intent of her wickedness, and received it only in his vest. Brunchilda was once again secured; and they all left the apartment they were then in to see her conveyed to her prison, excepting Count Richard, the son of Grodern, and the armed appearance.

Having seen Brunchilda safely secured in her chamber, the Duke returned to the imprisoned Count; but he found him alone and in a swoon. In this situation he thought proper to leave him, and, locking the door, rejoined the stranger knight, who had remained with Hildegarde to protect her from injury.

The remainder of the day passed off in converse on the past: it was resolved that the wicked Duchess should that night remain where she was, as Albert had given orders for some new alteration in the chambers allotted to his lady in the haunted wing, which would render them more secure from both internal and external attacks. In the evening, one of her guards came to inform the Duke that his lady had lost her reason.

"That has long, I apprehend, been the case," said Grimoald; "but let us now visit her, lest this should be more of feigned insanity than real."

Albert arose; and they all went to see her: they found her in a high delirious fever, and plainly perceived she was too ill for design. The tide of passion had been too impetuous, it had rushed over her soul and borne away reason in its course. Pity, for a while, now took place of indignation in the bosom of the mild Albert: he ordered her chains to be taken from her, and every assistance procured which could remove her disorder, until the return of health should render her able to support her punishment. His compassion proved her death, for, in one of her delirious moments, she started from her attendants and ran from the room, the door of which had been left open to admit a free circulation of the air:—coming to some stone-steps, she threw herself to the bottom, and dashed her brains out.—The amiable Hildegarde shed many tears for the sad fate of her mother: it was not her loss she mourned, but her method of departure and her wicked life. To Albert, both were matters of more deep reflection than he had ever known; and he retired for a few hours to a solitary apartment to indulge in solemn thought.

Another dreadful night now passed over the detestable Hubert, whom for the future we will never call Count Richard, as the real Count is here. 'When sable night each weary wight restor'd,' brought on the terrors of the wicked, and was far advanced, the door of Hubert's chamber flew open, and six figures in black, each bearing a discipline in one hand and a taper in the other, entered: they were followed by the son of Grodern and the real Count Richard, bearing in a ghastly shattered and bloody figure, in whose mangled features Hubert seemed to behold the bad Brunchilda.—Frozen with horror, he neither spoke nor moved—the colour fled from his visage, and his hair arose; whilst the spirit of Brunchilda thus addressed him:—"It is not for us, oh Hubert, to arise from the regions of damnation and declare the mysteries of our lot, or describe the manner of our punishments, yet great and heavy is the latter; and were we not past from the bodies of mortality, and were

only souls that never die, it would extinguish our existence: but we must bear immeasurable sufferings; for we
never are impaired or can decay, but are every hour
more susceptible of pain! We were warned before our
departure, but we scorned to consider; and we are forced
to own at once the justice and power of God! We are
not sent hither to declare the crimes of others, but to
warn the wicked, and force the guilty sinner to repentance. But thou, my brother, not alone so by blood but
in atrocious deeds, wilt not confess thy crimes to relieve
the innocent or betray the guilty: thou wilt not repent;
yet thou shalt confess, and to betray thyself!—the Duke
approaches, give him thy deposition!!!"

At that minute the Duke and Grimoald entered the
apartment; they beheld Brunchilda, and they heard her
speak, with an amazement past description.—"Now
then, Count Richard," she continued, "take down the
catalogue of his sins." Hubert was silent! One of the
figures, in black, advanced, and gave him a flagellation,
after having ordered the Count and Grodern's son to
divest him of all his upper garments:—he still remained
in silent sullenness! The second figure then approached,
and, assisted by the first, applied the discipline. It was in
vain; Hubert would not speak by either threats or execution, although every one had played their part until the
blood ran down the sides and shoulders of the sullen
wight: malice gave him a courage equal to it all.—Bring
forth the rack, said the armed Count.—Four men entered, and the rack was brought. Hubert shuddered at
the sight, whilst the Duke regarded in speechless wonder.

"Now, Hubert, wilt thou confess?" asked Richard's ghost.

His tongue now performed its office, and he growled out, 'never.'—Waste no more time, but bind him on, did Count Richard say; and they immediately seized the lacerated body of Hubert, and made him fast to the rack, and proceeded to inflict the merited reward of such unparalleled obstinacy. The agony this occasioned was too much for the guilty soul of Hubert: he sunk beneath the pangs, his courage was no more, and he called out to Albert to spare him further torment, for he would relate all he knew. Being unbound, he found himself too much exhausted to perform his promise, and therefore intreated a respite until the ensuing day. This was with some difficulty granted. The ghost of Richard then advised the Duke to quit those apartments entirely, until he attended again for the recital of Hubert. Albert complied, and took the stranger with him: Grimoald was vexed at this. He requested permission to remain and watch the apparitions. Count Richard overheard him, and, laying his hand on the knight's shoulder, said, I would warn you against impertinent curiosity, unless you have any particular desire to undergo a flagellation like what we have bestowed on Hubert. Albert laughed at the condition to which this reduced Grimoald; who certainly showed very visible signs of fear, and yet scorned to own he was afraid; and therefore began to threaten the insolent apparitions with instant demolition. However, in pity, he insisted on his accompanying him back; which Grimoald was obliged to comply with; and they returned to the favourite hall of Hildegarde, where they found her and Raymond, who was listening to the music of her harp. The young lady, on seeing her father, put it aside, whilst she listened to his account of the sable spirits: at the end of which Raymond could not avoid rallying Grimoald for his courage. The Avenger seemed not very much pleased at his mirth, and, to end it, requested the lady to continue her music. Having complied with his petition, the harp went round. Raymond and Albert both understood its use; but their performance was frequently interrupted by the remarks of the Avenger, who would also occasionally clear his voice as if preparing to sing. Raymond observed it, and privately gave a hint to Hildegarde not to ask him. Albert gave the stranger the harp, and carelessly asked him to perform: he made instantly very double-faced refusals, asserting he did not understand it: and when he did play, he only did so from his own ideas and words. Albert, who was thinking of many other things, very readily took his refusal. Grimoald still held the instrument. A fresh conversation was commenced, in which he took no part, until tired out, he said, My Lord, to convince you how very bad a performer I really am, I will give you a specimen of my minstrelsy; but I assure you, I comply with pain.

Albert had been so deeply engaged in conversation, that he only heard the last words of Grimoald, and exclaimed, "Bless me, Sir knight, what is it you are going to do? 'To play, my lord.' "For Heaven's sake, Sir knight, do not put yourself to any pain, I beg," said Raymond. 'Oh, I must certainly oblige you,' replied he.—Without giving them time to say another word, he began to run his voice up and down the gamut, striking the chords violently at the same time, which having done, he sung

Hark, the tempests of the north
Split their caves and sally forth:
Rocky fragments up they tear;
High aloft their spoil they bear;
Howling, rend the trembling air;
Whizzing from the earth they fly,
Dash the clouds and bruise the sky.

You see, said Grimoald, when he finished, how poor a minstrel I am! but the words are my own. You may discover, no doubt, how much I despise low ideas and love-sick poetry: the grand, the sublime, alone pleases me.

Yes, replied Raymond; but your tempests are so boisterous, that the sky seems to want a plaster after their expeditions, to heal the bruises.

As for that, said Grimoald, laying his head aside, with two little nods of inexpressible self-complacency, I have had an idea I assure you of soothing the sorrows of oppressed nature: I have descended to the tender and pathetic, somewhat mixed with the sublime; and have sung as follows:—

The sympathetic clouds draw near;
The sorrows of the sky they hear;
Grow black with grief and lend a tear.
They bid the tempests cease to growl;
They bid the wild winds stay their howl;
They call the fleecy aid of snows,
And tenderly wrap up the blows.

On the morrow they attended to hear the confession of Hubert; but they found him returned to his dear loved obstinacy. The rack was again brought; but the sight was sufficient this time to conquer him; for, turning to Albert, he addressed him as follows:—

Now hearken, and let thy harrowed soul glut itself with the full cup of bitterest anguish: but to pierce thy heart still deeper, I must carry my recital back as far as the time of Brunchilda's mother.

Ludovicus lived happy and contented with his first princess; his subjects were obedient, his neighbours at peace with him, and his wife every thing that was amiable. Soon after their union, a daughter was born to them; excellent and amiable as the mother, although not equally beautiful. The annals of history could not produce an instance of three people more universally respected and beloved, nor could the records of family-felicity show any more happy. Compare my recital with thy lot, oh prince, and grind thy teeth! let the contrast awake every feeling yet dormant. Such was the case of Ludovicus until he first beheld Gunilda: the attractions of this princess obliterated the less novel ones of his wife, who, hurt by the difference of his behaviour, and finding every effort to regain his tenderness in vain, sunk into a melancholy, which absorbed her spirits and her health. She ceased to try for love, and only lived to anguish. Little could she wish to frequent those scenes which only reminded her of instances of past felicity, and presented those of present grief. The company of her husband could give only pain; for then she beheld the wiles of Gunilda successfully exerted. She shunned, therefore, the society of Ludovicus, and buried herself in the recesses of her chamber. Gunilda took advantage of her absence, and tried to awaken the jealousy of her paramour: she painted the conduct of the injured wife in colours of the darkest hue; and taught Ludovicus to fancy hatred and illicit affection made his wife shun his sight. No longer the respectful lover or the tender husband, he became suspicious, rough, ill-tempered, and unfeeling. It was too much for his amiable consort; long had she been declining: at length sorrow and the pangs of child-birth ended her life; but her infant lived, and proved a son.

Almost sooner than decency or any attention to common opinion and the usual general form would admit, Ludovicus married the infamous Gunilda, who had then two children living; who were Brunchilda and myself. The son of the departed princess, my mother determined to bring up herself, and, for that purpose, had him conveyed to her own suite of apartments; and no person, but such as she approved, was suffered to approach him: all the old attendants were removed, and the adherants of Gunilda became his nurses and her slaves. A short time elapsed, when a report was spread through the palace of his death. She had ordered two of her people to murder him, and prepare every thing with decency for the eye of her husband, should he desire to view the dead body of the infant.

Ludovicus felt much affliction at the news; his little son was dear to him. Gunilda had attempted to persuade him it was not his own; but her malicious insinuations gained no ground, and he rejected them with contempt. He had not been long united to my mother before the virtues of his deceased princess arose before his memory, and every day gleamed with more vivid lustre: the vices of Gunilda awakened agonies in his bosom, and the contrast grew powerful. He asked to see his dead son; and, to prevent suspicion, was gratified in his desire. A blackness round the throat of the infant attracted his attention: he demanded the reason. Gunilda was vexed at the carelessness of the murderers, who had not done their business to her wishes, but had left this sign of violence upon him; but she struggled with her anger, and hid her confusion whilst she informed the unfortunate father that his son had died in violent convulsions.

Ludovicus felt unsatisfied; appearances were strange, and he ordered an examination to take place: but so well had the vile woman contrived, and so very corrupt were most who surrounded their master, that they pretended and declared there appeared nothing but what was the natural consequences of convulsive fits. The mind of Ludovicus remained unsatisfied; but, with sorrow, at last he was obliged to resign the body to the grave, and himself to composure.

Not long after this affair, some words happening between my mother and those of her agents who had dispatched the young prince, a great coolness ensued between them. Gunilda seemed never easy; rest was banished from her mind; and she soon found it necessary to banish from her court the objects of her care. The two men were suddenly missing: little enquiry was made after them, being neither beloved nor valued; and the conversation on their departure soon died away. I fancied to myself, and do not now doubt it, that Gunilda had poisoned them, or otherwise contributed to their deaths: but the matter was too quickly hushed up for discovery to be made.

My mother was not yet at rest: a being still remained obnoxious to her peace: one who had a superior claim to the affection of Ludovicus, and who also might hereafter stand in the way of her ambition. This was the daughter of the departed princess, and sister of the murdered prince.

Murder might appear too glaring when perpetrated on so old a person, and the trouble infinitely greater; and the more so, because that princess was not so much under her care. She turned her aim, therefore, to the driving her from the castle, by rendering her life miserable.

Emma (for that was her name) had married secretly a young nobleman, who visited at the court of her father; and in the affection of Etheburt she sought relief from the sorrows of her heart. The marriage was soon by Gunilda's spies discovered, and the consequence was loss of liberty to Emma, and of life to her spouse. After his death the world had no joys for her, especially the scenes of a corrupted court. Ludovicus made her an offer of freedom, which she only accepted until she could take the veil, and forever resign a public station; but lest the malice of Gunilda should still follow her, she threw herself into some distant convent, and was never again heard of.

Many people looked gloomy at Emma's absence; and suspicion rested on my mother; but knowing most of her actions, I could very well acquit her of this offence which was supposed: Emma had actually retired, and may now be living: but of that I solemnly protest I know not.

Gunilda, whose whole soul was vice, could not very long continue satisfied with the love of Ludovicus. It could not be expected that a woman who had dared to carry on an intrigue with the husband of another, should long continue faithful to her own, although that own had been the object of her unworthy love. Every handsome courtier was obliged to yield to her passion, or find banishment reward his contempt.

At length Count Richard came.—Let me not be obliged to recite his murder, it harrows up my soul; let me only declare that these are the chambers of assassination. Ludovicus was then absent. On his return to the court she invented the most infamous tales about him, and declared he had retreated from thence, fearing the just anger of his prince. She prayed I might be invested with his dignity, and enriched with all his possessions; and, to familiarize his vassals to me, I assumed his name; nor were any suffered to call me otherwise but on pain of death.

On the morning after Count Richard was destroyed, my mother shut up his apartments: but we were not safe throughout the whole wing from terrors of our conscience: the day was gloomy, and at night imagination or reality presented to our startled views some ghastly spectre; the place became insufferable, and the whole side seemed haunted.

One evening, in a fit of horror, we arose from table, and leaving every thing as it was, caused the wing immediately to be closed up forever. When Ludovicus returned (for this also happened during his absence) he was pleased we had left these apartments, which are by far the most unpleasant in the castle, and always disliked by him. His enquiries, therefore, on the change were but trifling; and he never counterordered the commands of Gunilda; on which account they were never again opened until the present time.

On your marriage with Brunchilda, I obtained your consent to reside as formerly in your court; but your permission did not make me your friend. No; sovereignty was my wish, and I envied your possessions. I have exerted every power to render you detested; for scarcely was there a wife, daughter, or sister of any poor vassal in your domains, but what I have drawn into my wiles, and made the villany pass for yours. The lovely, the innocent Dunisleda baffled me by flight. The first attack was but a sham one, with no further design than to have made her a prisoner, to get her conveyed to the castle: where she would have long continued wholly in my power.—Curse on thy folly which has counteracted the designs of my revenge, and has given freedom and happiness to the objects of my anger.—Like her mother, Brunchilda had a roving disposition; and yet I often believe it was more from the love of wrong than the love of variety, that every stranger was preferred to thee. What could be the attractions of the clownish peasant? yet such were frequently thy rivals. The handsome son of Grodern whom thou knowest so superior to all his associates, whose countenance displays such intelligence and greatness, and his manner such dignity, him she loved beyond all other beings; but he despised her.—The saucy peasant shunned her allurements, and dared to fix his fancy on thy Hildegarda: she returned his love: fair, unspotted virgin! thy age's hope, thy bosom's comfort! your virtuous maiden! How often have I seen her retire into the forest, to spend the day in wanton dalliance with the humble cottager!—"Hush! hold thy execrable tongue," exclaimed the Duke, "dare not to defame my daughter!"—Nay, Duke, I will proceed. I will not defame thy virtuous daughter. Why sendest thou not for thy two little grandsons who reside with Jacquemar? Did not the son of Grodern wish to see his infants nursed? Did not he place them near at hand? How pleasant were the stolen interviews of the fond parents, when together they would visit the cottage, and embrace their offspring! Oh, as a parent, thou must feel,—how sweet to caress an innocent child!—Ah, I see thou feelest.'

"Vile calumniator," said the Duke, falling overpowered with anguish into the arms of an attendant.—Oh, continued the execrable Hubert, let not thy grief be great; remove thy fear; her love was not lavished on him alone; many a knight has shared her favour.—As for me, I loved her not, I hated her; I hated thee. How did my soul pant for a torture to bestow on thee! how did I wish that, after her being some time subdued to my power, she should bring forth an offspring to call thee grandpapa,—me uncle, father, all at once.—how it would have cheered thy aged heart! Sweet social compact, endearing double tie:—Thus might Hubert have ran on to eternity. Albert could hear no more.—Why did he credit such a miscreant! but who can account for parental feelings! the sudden shock!—Wound up to the nicest pitch, they are all harmony: strike them with too rude a hand, they snap, and discord must succeed.—

Long, in vain, did his attendants strive to comfort him. At length his Hildegarde, led by the son of Grodern, came to seek her father. Just then reanimation had began to illuminate his visage; just then he began to discredit the vile reciter: but, just then, he beheld his daughter accompanied by the peasant's son! To sorrow rage succeeded; and the once gentle Albert drove them from his presence with the fury of the wildest maniac; he drew his sword, and tried to pursue them through the wing; but his progress was interrupted by the arm of Count Richard.—"Pursue them, pursue them," said the Duke, his eyes nearly starting from their sockets with increasing anger; "they have escaped."

Count Richard at this suffered him to proceed, and followed his hasty steps, unknowing whom he should pursue; but fancying it was Hubert.—Hildegarde escaped to her chamber, whither the astonished son of Grodern followed, ignorant of the place to which she led him, but anxious to protect her. The Duke soon entered. His daughter had fainted and fallen on the ground. By her had sunk on one knee the innocent intentioned Edgar; and was supporting her head upon his bosom. Albert, stung to madness by the sight, aimed a furious blow at him; but the blindness of his rage made him miss the object, and he fell in the attempt; for his foot had lost its place, and his sword dropt from his hand; the leg of a couch received his head, and a violent blow, in consequence, deprived him of all sensation.—For a few moments surprise suspended every power in both Richard and young Edgar; but at length the former recovered his recollection, and summoned the Duke's attendants; with whose assistance he conveyed the body of Albert to his own apartment, where Richard left him and returned to Hildegarde, who had once recovered, but had relapsed again, immediately that recollection of the mournful cause awoke to weigh down sense. Grief and horror made her for many days unable to leave her chamber; but the mystery was quickly cleared by those who had been present at the wicked recital of the malicious Hubert. After some time Albert began to recover; but it was very slowly. The blow received in the fall was not alone the cause of his disorder; it was augmented by the agitation he had undergone during some of the late transactions at the castle, but most especially on the tale of Hubert. The two knights and Richard made him perceive his error; and to rage, sorrow for the suffering of his Hildegarde succeeded. One day, suddenly rousing himself, he cried in a quick embittered accent, Oh tell me, tell me, how came she with that youth! If you can bear continued surprise, I will prove she is innocent, and that Edgar is worthy of her love, said the Count steadily.—Albert bowed assent, and Richard continued:—I will for a few hours depart; let the wicked Hubert be brought hither, and the father of the young man shall give you satisfaction.—Richard then departed, and Albert sent for his daughter. The weak condition of Hildegarde subjected her to a fainting fit. Joy was a while too much; but by evening they were recovered. At seven a knock was heard at the door of Albert's apartment: the Duke ordered it to be opened; and directly entered the ghost of Brunchilda, supported by Grodern and his son: then the stranger knight; and next Hubert, attended by Sir Raymond and two old men.—Albert commanded the parties to be seated; and Grodern thus began:—"Albert, thou hast been imposed on: the story of that monster is false. Perhaps thou expectest the approach of Richard to give thee the promised discovery:—Other Richard than is present is there none.—Grodern rising, threw off the peasant's habit, and Count Richard appeared. He continued: "Hubert, thy arts succeeded not; I swallowed not thy poison. Thy mother turned the court into a scene of revelry and wantonness: in such a court, with such a mother, what could Brunchilda be?—Thou and thy sister were ever wicked.—The vile affections of thy mother were turned on me. Duty to my prince, the memory of his departed wife, every thing spoke against my favouring her illicit passion; but, above all, my detestation of her conduct steeled my heart. Who can love a bold woman? Every step a female makes from modesty, is two to drive us back. Time made me settle my affection on a beautiful foreigner, and I married her publicly. My prince was not displeased; but Gunilda's love turned to hatred: my offence was unpardonable. She told Ludovicus my marriage was against his interest, my wife and her attendants were spies from the enemy, and that I carried on seditious purposes.—Let us only then do good answered Ludovicus, so only good shall be reported.—This was all the effect of her insinuations. Vexation and disappointment augmented her revenge; and nothing but my death would now appease her. I contrived to send my wife from court, determining to follow her the first moment I was enabled. One night, in the palace, I was awakened from my sleep by an attempt made at the door of my chamber to force it open. I called out, and was answered that it was a message of consequence: I therefore suffered the person to enter; but, to my surprise, he was followed by Gunilda and her son Hubert, completely armed: they rushed in, and immediately murdered my servant.—I was totally unguarded. Hubert advanced with a poniard in his hand.—Now Sir, said he, take the reward of your perfidy.—Now villain, said Gunilda, prepare to die, in recompense for the guilt my incredulous husband refused to punish.—Alas! madam, said I, wherein has my crime consisted?—Drink this poison first, and then your conscience will cry out in bitter accents when the pangs of death approach, replied Hubert, presenting me a cup.—Wretch, said Gunilda, have you not attempted my honour? My son, we will be our own avengers; force him to swallow the beverage of death.—I then appealed to the son:—Alas! Sir, I am innocent: you, madam, know it full well.— Transported with fury at my delay, and fearing I should betray to Hubert her own guilt, she snatched at the poniard, but I prevented her, by crying out, "No madam, I am willing to die, in preference to living under so base, so false an accusation:—give me the poisoned cup."— Hubert gave it me, I seemed to drink the mixture; but I contrived to pour a great part over my bosom. Some I was obliged to swallow; and so counterfeited the effects of nausea, that, seeing my lips wet, they concluded I had drank sufficient. When Hubert gave me the cup, the light shone on the silver bottom, and discovered to me the settlement which delay had caused. In shaking my hand, to imitate trembling, I took care not to raise the noxious dregs. My precautious saved my life. From the little which had gone down, I felt great heat; wherefore grinding my teeth as if in agony, I placed one hand on my stomach, and with the other dashed the cup from me.—They staid to see the effect; and supposing I was greatly hurt, they exclaimed, "this works well. Such be the reward of traitors!" They then left me, in what they supposed a fainting fit, and fastened the door. When morning drew near, and but few of the domestics were stirring, I took my departure, unperceived by any but the porter of the castle, whom I bribed to be silent on the subject. Sometime before this happened, I had discovered a secret pannel in my chamber; which was loose; and on removing it, found behind it a passage which went straight under the river to the convent, and ended in a cell, where its opening was hidden by some wood made to resemble stone; and against that was placed an altar, with a crucifix. Before I departed, I procured a large chest from the convent, and dragging the body of my servant down, I deposited it therein.

After my escape, from the castle, having procured an entire disguise, I entered the convent, and, through the cell, visited the chambers of the castle, which I had left, and found them in the same state I left them. The passage I found communicated with every part of the building; by which discovery I contrived to terrify the guilty Gunilda continually, until I caused the whole wing to be deserted. I then left them entirely, having founded a strong presumption of ghosts in the castle, and joined my Countess. The morning after the supposed perpetration of her crime, Gunilda sent for the porter of the castle, and gave him a very large sum to say he had seen me depart early in the morning.—The man was much surprised, and took the money, but never informed her I had really done so. On the return of

Ludovicus, she told him I had attempted by violence to dishonour her; but she had been saved by Hubert.

My wife was at another court. On my joining her, we changed our names:—we had nothing left of our property, but what we had in specie or jewels. To Hubert were all my possessions given; and those of my wife were lost in war. We converted what we could into money, and assuming the habits of peasants, came and settled in the forest, waiting for time's enabling us to punish villany. Our son, by his labour, helped to support us; and had not designs been carried to the wicked length they have, we might have retained our simple appearance until our deaths, as we had enjoyed so much satisfaction and content in our quiet retreat. Curiosity sometimes led me to pass through the passages of the castle; and thence was I enabled to learn the wickedness of Brunchilda, and in some measure to counteract her designs. Thus have I been no ghost;—but I believed there remained no hopes of conquering thy wicked machinations, unless by something marvellous.—Oh, Hubert, thou shouldst be brought to confession. I was passing to the Duke's chamber when I heard the screams of Hildegarde, and starting through the pannel, whilst thy back was turned, thy wicked conscience might well surprise thee into the belief of my being more than mortal.—So certain it is there never existed a ghost yet, but in an overcharged conscience, or a weak mind. The foolish and wicked impose upon the unlearned, and teach them to believe every tale of superstition.

The skeleton which gave Duke Albert and his party such surprise, was but my murdered servant's. By cords and springs I brought it to act as was seen: a matter easy to invention; and the doors which they went through that night were made like stone, not to be discovered on the outside.—Let the supposed ghost of Brunchilda unmask.

This was done, and they beheld the abbess of the convent: she was no other than the Princess Emma, who had always been reckoned very like Brunchilda: the same size and shape rendered the deception easy.—Here Grimoald interposed:—"Let the auditors of Count Richard prepare for a new cause of wonder:—In me behold the son of Ludovicus and his Annasleda:—a child was substituted in my place, and I was conveyed away. Providence gave my preservers wherewith to support me; and they kept from me the knowledge of my birth. Fidelity and arms made them think me proper to be entrusted with the secret; and on hearing it I came hither, on pretence of seeking adventures. Thus these domains are mine."—The Duke looked angry, vexed, surprized; but Count Richard prevented a reply by speaking thus:—'No, boaster, no; thou art nothing: it is I alone can produce the real heir. Step forward Edgar; come hither my friends.'—Edgar and the old men arose and came forward.—They declared they were those employed by Gunilda to murder the young prince, but had other designs in view; and had, by the direction of the Count, preserved his life and placed the dead infant for inspection. The blackness on his neck was stained in, to deceive Gunilda.—'Hubert,' said Count Richard, 'tell us, Are not these the men thy mother set to perform the deed?'

"Nothing would make me own the truth of what I am so much surprised to see," replied the monster, "but

114

the spite I bear Albert. In Edgar's countenance I have
long remarked a likeness of his father, and hated him for
it." The Count continued, for surprise had made Albert
silent.—'I have watched over his infancy with the greatest care; and he is worthy of his birth. It was I who sent
him to guard the young lady at the time you was so
much enraged. Long have they loved each other; and
both are virtuous. When he worked in the gardens he
was often with her; but they never strayed from the
paths of rectitude. Often would she visit my ancient
Countess; and knew my son (for I ever beheld him as
such) was of no peasant birth. Duty to thee made her
strive to conquer her innocent passion, and forget her
Edgar; but it has now returned with greater ardor.' Albert sighed: but suddenly arose, and presented Edgar
with the hand of Hildegarde, overwhelming them both
with joy, astonishment, and confusion.—"My children,"
said he, "these territories are now yours; I have only to
resign them, and to wish you happy." Edgar threw himself at the feet of Albert:—'No, Sire, whilst you live, they
shall have no other master: your daughter is all I covet:
let us reside in your castle, blessed with your protection;
but more we wish not. This was seconded by his daughter and the Count; and at length obtained the reluctantly
given consent of the Duke. They now turned to the
other parties, but one was gone; Grimoald had departed,
perhaps to show his courage on some tamer beings.
Contempt was all that followed him.

Hubert was confined for life, and his possessions
bestowed where merit claimed the preference: a portion
was given to Jacquemar and his infants. The union of
Edgar was completed with his Hildegarde; and joy began

once more to irradiate the dwelling of Duke Albert: Sir Raymond soon after departed for England; and through this means we have been furnished with the particulars of the foregoing story.

THE END.

Notes

1   *the sweet and alluring recitals of a Reeve, a White, or a
    Lee...a Smollet, a Hume, or a Rapin:* Clara Reeve (1729-
    1807) was the author of the hugely influential Gothic
    novel *The Old English Baron* (1778). James White was
    the author of several popular historical novels, including
    Earl Strongbow (1789) and *John of Gaunt* (1790). The sis-
    ters Sophia and Harriet Lee were prolific writers at the
    end of the eighteenth century. Sophia Lee's *The Recess;
    or a Tale of Other Times* (1783-85) was an early and im-
    portant Gothic novel; *The Canterbury Tales*, on which
    the two sisters collaborated, was extremely popular and
    remained in print throughout the nineteenth century.
    Tobias Smollett (1721-1771) was one of the first great
    English novelists, and author of such works as *Roderick
    Random* (1748) and *The Expedition of Humphrey Clinker*
    (1771). David Hume (1711-1776) was an important
    Enlightenment philosopher and author of *An Enquiry
    Concerning Human Understanding* (1739-40). Paul de
    Rapin (1661-1725) was a French historian who wrote an
    early and influential history of England.
    Recess: an early historical Gothic novel by Sophia Lee,
    published in 1783-85.

2   *Hugh Capet:* early French king (987-96) and founder of
    the Capetian dynasty.

17 *"But ah! what pain..."*: William Lisle Bowles, "Sonnet
    XIII" (1789) (slightly misquoted).

CPSIA information can be obtained
at www.ICGtesting.com
Printed in the USA
FSOW01n1321270716
23167FS